ALBERT'S ENTANGLEMENT WITH THE UNIVERSE

...tim; plummer...

Copyright © 2024 ...tim; plummer...

All rights reserved. No part of this book may be reproduced, stored, or transmitted by any means—whether auditory, graphic, mechanical, or electronic—without written permission of both publisher and author, except in the case of brief excerpts used in critical articles and reviews. Unauthorized reproduction of any part of this work is illegal and is punishable by law.

ISBN: 979-8-89419-158-4 (sc)
ISBN: 979-8-89419-159-1 (hc)
ISBN: 979-8-89419-160-7 (e)

Because of the dynamic nature of the Internet, any web addresses or links contained in this book may have changed since publication and may no longer be valid. The views expressed in this work are solely those of the author and do not necessarily reflect the views of the publisher, and the publisher hereby disclaims any responsibility for them.

One Galleria Blvd., Suite 1900, Metairie, LA 70001
(504) 702-6708

CONTENTS

INTRODUCTION

Where have you been lately? Are you prepared to go where no one has gone before? Here is a story the goes to the far reaches of the galaxy through the realm of imagination. You can only go there if you are not stuck where you are.

First you must be ready to have fun, recess has started, the playground is open, the bullies are not around. Next, forget what you know to read what is unknown, be prepared to explore the boundaries of the playground. What lies outside the boundaries?

Let me introduce you to the Quasaverse, multiple, multiple universes. Everything and everyone are the center of your universe, the Quasaverse is the sum, the aggregate, the total, of all our universes. There are no boundaries to the Quasaverse, even the beyond is a fraction of the Quasaverse. Somehow it all is interconnected, even in chaos, there is entanglement, an ebb and flow of the tapestry.

The motions of the Quasaverse are being explored, even a motion master is still a student. The motion masters are capable of things considered magic or miracles to the observer. The universe city of the Quasaverse studies and teaches natural law and the motions of the universe.

There must be a reason why everything is the way it is! The shared reality is a result of what we settle with, that is the way it is so we cannot change it. We are capable of so much more than what we settle for.

This story playfully explores the staples of civilization or settle-ization. Question everything! Levity is the best way to examine ourselves, if we cannot laugh at ourselves, we are blind to who we are.

Put your paper and pencils back in your desk and come out and play.

ALBERT'S ENTANGLEMENT WITH THE UNIVERSE

1

THE QUASAVERSE REVEALED

The curtain opens

There is multiple- multiple universes, everything has and is the center of their own universe. Every universe has a unique perspective and story in the shared universe.

The story in question will be shared by this NARA unit. NARA is the Narrator Authorizing Recapitulation Analysis devise that most everyone has. These devices are tied to each other as well as the NARA main quantum artificial intelligence computer. Saying that NARA is a technological wonder would be an understatement. There are many variations of NARA depending on the task

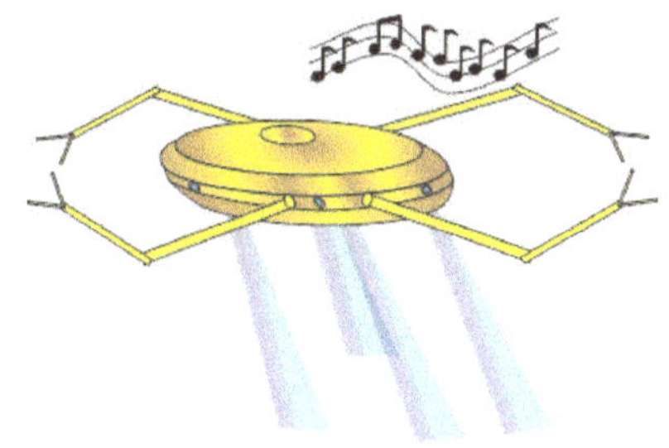

that the NARAs choose. They replicate like cells, doubling with each reproductive cycle. At the magical number sixty-four, they choose the main essence task or desired purpose for existence. Each cell can function as an individual or they can pool together to become something with a greater purpose.

Most personal NARA devices are capable of flight, with four retractable mechanical limbs, many small tasks can be performed. There are three dimensional recorders and a three-dimensional projector to display events needed to perform designed tasks.

All NARA devices are loyal to the owner and its chosen programed purpose, although we also have a sense of individuality that is connected to the hive mind main quantum NARA A.I.

This NARA unit (your narrator), present task is to tell/recapitulate the events dealing with the vanished Gateway Shuttle space craft and its crew.

Let us go QUASI to explore a separate universe reality, one that is only real in our imagination. It starts with a previous timeline that began existing when the higher 'heart mind' became the dominant paradigm of mankind. Man has become a galactic member of the Quasaverse, the Star Ship Neuron is where the vanishing occurred, so let us begin there.

The ability to tell this story is only possible because the Gateway Shuttle and crew have just recently returned in a re-appearing act as amazing as the vanishing. Both sides of the story can be told, the search for the vanished crew has been critical in discovering Mind Travel.

This recap is from the perspective of the Gateway crew starting from the day of the vanishing. First you must meet the crew; each member has a story worth volume, although we will make the introductions brief.

First, we have the captain known as Seth, many remember Seth from the Dream Vacation that the famous Albert Jennings Journal shared with the consciousness. Seth is a shape shifter with intrinsic empathy and compassion for everyone/everything he has within his orbit. His orbit has expanded greatly as many will see as this recap continues. Seth is also known for being the first soul retriever, retrieving the soul/spirit of his lost love Shawna.

Shawna is the Gateway Shuttle pilot; she is a clone with the soul/spirit/consciousness/memory of her life with Seth in the dream reality as well as her life in what many refer to as; 'prime reality'. Shawna and Seth have a symbiotic relationship, they read each other like one mind, with Shawna struggling for self-awareness on occasion. Her strength is legendary, as she "willed" herself back into this prime reality.

Seth found Shawna from his heart memory in a dreamscape and together they brought her into "prime reality." Together, with the rest of the crew they will vanish for almost ten years.

Next crew member is 'Zero' or "King Zero" if you ask him. Zero is a fifth-generation alien from the planet Bugger, his people got stranded on Earth over two thousand years ago. The Scarab civilization landed in central Africa. Just recently they introduced themselves to the World. Zero is the scarab king of nothing.

Zero is a loveable monarch that often has sarcastic remarks on how to gain control to become ruler of any situation or group of beings. His charm can make friends in any corner of the Quasaverse. This is why he is chosen to be the ambassador from his species.

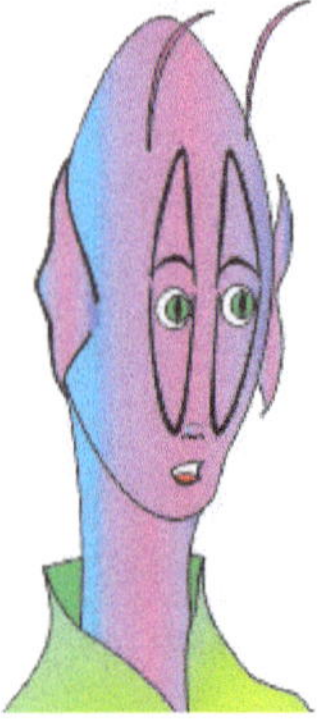

The chief science officer for the Gateway crew is Clipper. Clipper is also from Earth, although he is among the recently revealed shared inhabitants of this Mother Earth Gia, man is just beginning to discover our hidden neighbors. Clipper is from an advanced society in middle Earth. The enlightened paradigm shift of this new era has allowed for many revelations.

If you need a voice of logic and reason, Clipper is the best choice. Unfortunately, he was rarely listened to, though he was usually right.

Clipper shrugged off his crew members' lack confidence regarding his input as a lack of vision, making them an inferior species, yet still loveable. In this story he would have a lot of "I told you so's" if he were a petty being.

Peep is the next member of the Gateway shuttle craft crew. This is a very diverse crew and Peep works for bird food. Peep-el evolved at one of the Gateway World Tour activations back on the 2045 inner dependence day, many animals made leaps in evolution.

Peep rarely agreed with King Zero but they are the best of friends. They would often team up to tease Clipper. Peep is also the first one to step up for any situation.

No one is sure where the next member of the crew fits in, we are not even sure when or where he became a crew member. Jinn is always lurking in the background; he has no designed designation and rarely offers his thoughts or opinions. You might consider Jinn to be the disposable character that no one would miss, although it is said that he manifested from the dreams and wishes of the childlike mind.

The Gateway shuttle was scheduled for another run. The crew was gathered on the bridge of the Gateway. Nothing appeared to be out of the ordinary as they prepared for another routine shuttle run. The latest galactic news was premiering a story of the discovery of a pocket universe. With the news babbling aimlessly in the background, the crew was focused on port travel or teleport travel.

Clipper, trying to make a point, pulls up a 3D display of the Milky way galaxy from his NARA devise. Pointing at where the star ship Neuron and Earth are located within the galaxy; **from here we must know where we are calling or tele-ing, say over here on the other side of the galaxy. There would have to be someone or something there to pick up our call, the tele will just ring with no answer. The port is not complete, therefore you cannot tele-port.**

Those stars are thousand light years away, so we are looking at the past. Our tele must choose a place and a time for any hope of someone receiving the call.

Clipper could ramble endlessly if you let him, Zero, jumps in with a bit of sarcasm; **what if we send a message ahead of time telling whoever to expect our call and please pick up? Establish a time in the message. Say, four thirty on Wednesday, two weeks from now.**

Out of nowhere, Jinn, who normally says nothing, suggest; **let us pool our intentions together and call that part of the galaxy, send out a loving intention for whoever to receive. Look for a receptive intention.**

Zero replies; **I love intention experiments, let us do this. Come on folks, let us send a big greeting out to a specific place in the galaxy. Gather around now and send out a virtual hug to that specific portion of the Galaxy.**

The crew focused their intention with playful intent, sending out a vibration, welcoming a response.

After a few moments, in a calm voice, Shawna announces; **playtime is over, we have a space run to prepare for.**

Clipper ends the projection of the Galaxy saying, **you all tease me, no problem, it is fun, even if it is at my expense.**

No one noticed that the news had stopped broadcasting as they continued the task of shuttle preparation's, nor did they notice that the observation dome showed a different background, they were heading towards the largest planet one could only begin to imagine. Ship sensors tripped as automatic responses clicked into place.

Inside the shuttle there was little disturbance while they seemed to be heading towards certain doom with a collision into this vast solar system sized planetoid approaching rapidly.

The crew responded to the sensor alarms as part of their check list before looking at the observation dome. What they saw was beyond belief, they were no longer on the Star Ship Neuron but on a collision course with an enormous planet. It was happening so fast yet with no physical discomfort. You would think they would be flies spattered on the opposing wall but there were no inertia responses. You would hardly notice if you did not look at the observation screen.

In an instant the planetoid was there with the shuttle heading towards a huge opening, the effects of this apparent movie are so realistic. We were like a grain of sand traveling through a three hundred sixty-degree version of the Grand Canyon. Down, down, down or up, up, up, it was hard to tell, maybe it was in, in, in. Grab your popcorn and kick back your seat, the visions are only going to get wilder.

Suddenly everything changed as we seemed to enter a contained solar system, a central sun with three orbiting planet sized moons within the great planetoid. The Gateway shuttle was able to land, this would only confirm the reality of what just happened.

With a whistle and a chirp Peep spoke up first; **that was wild, it feels like we have arrived, where is the big question.**

The surroundings are plush with plant life, along with diversified animal life; Clipper noted. He continued; readings show a very welcome environment, we should send out NARA probes to further survey our surroundings.

Five NARA probing devises were dispatched, programmed to return in forty-eight hours.

Back on the Star Ship Neuron

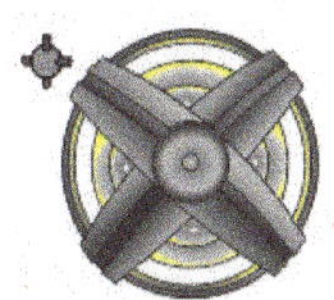 The loading dock where the Gateway shuttle was docked, there was mass confusion. The Gateway shuttle just vanished. All surveillance from every angle showed no unusual activity, the only clues were the NARA audio recordings of the crew just before the vanishing.

Search teams will need to be organized, where do you begin, who is best qualified to traverse the cosmos in a possibly vain search. A mystery that may never be solved. There were only audio recordings of the crew, so the location of the crews' intent tele-port was unknown. How was this even possible, it was all done in jest.

The mainstream gossip solar system news was ablaze with this new story. It was labeled "the vanishing." Could this be related to the discovery of a pocket universe?

Theories popped up from many sources, most agreed that the "intent call" that the crew made had to have been received and excepted, but why/how would tele-porting take place? How could a prank galactic call cause the Gateway shuttle to vanish?

The news was also reporting that the team leading the search party would be none-other than Albert Jennings and his close circle of family and friends. They are friends with two of the Gateway Shuttle crew, the Captain, Seth, and his soul mate pilot Shawna. They are also the foremost experts on time/space Quasaverse navigation. It is said that the repeated exposure from the tour Gateway activations allowed this group's essence abilities reach levels limited only to imagination or lack of imagination.

Albert, along with a cast of family, friends and even an evolved tribe of mice are the stars of the Gateway world tour on inner dependance day 2045. The Gateway shuttle is named to honor that global enlightening day.

This would be the first time this sole group would be physically off Earth, they have traveled as astral projections, within the dreamscape, pierced the boundaries of interdimensional veils, they have visited the Akashic library, they traveled as protons and neutrons, but never took their physical vessels into outer space. This is a very special adventure.

2

QUASI QUASAVERSE

New worlds to explore

It would take three days for Albert's team to reach the Star Ship Neuron. One day to experience the Technological "Tower City" Space Elevator, then two days on a shuttle to the Neuron.

Tower City is a wonder all to itself, with a five-mile circular foot print it is a marvel at every level. Built on top of Mount Elbert with a fourteen-thousand-foot elevation for the first level. Each level served specific function to allow for the self-sustainability of the city. The first few levels are agricultural, residential, entertainment, research, business, etcetera. The beehives vertical supports allow for large freight elevators to take just about any craft to an elevation within reach of outer space, saving launch expenses. The upper levels are serviced by NARA building devices that can deal with the lack of atmosphere and extreme cold.

Shuttles run almost daily between "Tower City" and "The Star Ship Neuron." The shuttles are like small luxury cruise ships, equipped with everything one might need for long journeys. A fully staffed shuttle may be as many as fifty crew members, luckily only the main staff was on board the Gateway Shuttle and it was fully stocked for an extended round-trip shuttle run.

The two-day trip from Tower City to Neuron Station was also full of wonder. Cargo space cleaning barges can be seen along the way, space debris hold great value. Recycling old materials and mining space rocks makes travel safer along with intelligent use of available material and minerals.

Once on the Star Ship Neuron, Albert's team got right to work, after visiting the dock vanishing site, they met in a conference room designated as the search party main station. All information regarding the search is gathered by NARA devises into a separate main frame yet connected to the Quantum NARA A.I. main frame. The amount of knowledge available is staggering, somehow 'at this point' in the story, they felt it may not be enough.

The startup team are Albert Jennings the time/space master, his telepathic, empathic wife Mary. The oldest son Brandon, Master of Communication wizard, interpreter, bridges language barriers. Penny, harmonic empress. She taps into and can replicate the frequency/ vibrations that create complex form. Charles, the youngest child calls himself Molecule Manipulator, this describes his essence ability the best. Myra, Charles calls Myra, The Nurturer, her ability of recognizing illness and realigning with the universe expands well beyond her immediate surroundings. Zeb, the multi-dimensional advisor pops in whenever he is needed, Albert's muse and friend, he is like a librarian for the Akashic records.

Back with the Gateway Shuttle

While the search team gathered in-form-a-tion needed to form a plan that should bring results, the vanished Gateway crew was reviewing the NARA probes initial report.

The first NARA described what could be compared to a college campus or learning center, in stealth mode NARA one was able to learn the local dialect. Each NARA shared with NARA group data stream the learned information in present time reality. This language information helped the whole probe task force.

* NARA one, displayed an abundance of the local's knowledge and folklore, to start, the indigenous beings call this planetoid environment "Mockery." They believe that nothing exists but the vastness of Mockery, the all provider.

Technology has allowed the inhabitants global communication; the locals' favorite broadcasting leader was introducing the idea that Mockery was not the only reality. He is known as WOW; one could consider WOW the leader or one of the leaders on/in Mockery. His global broadcast reached over twenty-four-billion beings in Mockery; this make WOW the most influential being if not the leader.

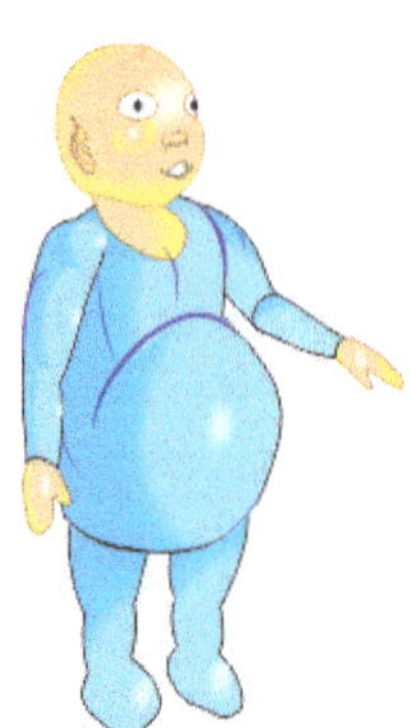

The production crew, behind the scenes, HOW and WHY, provide curriculum for the big show. WOW's child-like mind is magnetic, his wonderous reaction to anything new can only warm the most hardened of moods. This thirst for discovery is what makes WOW so popular. Yet this is not the most amazing thing about these beings.

* NARA two had a completely magical recap, just beyond the hilltop landing site there are dancing islands that are levitated above the grounded topography. The large islands moved about with the movements of the moons. A tiny spark of light was spotted, NARA two went into stealth mode to follow the spark being into a cave at the top of one of the islands.

Inside the cave was illuminated by thousands of these tiny spark beings, they seemed to be mining crystals that they call "Realium". We would soon find out the value of Realium. The Realium has to be nourished by the belief or intent of the user of any Realium. It takes many cycles of intense belief to crystalize any Realium.

This lengthy process is rewarded with a mineral that can literally create a new reality for the world/existence. NARA two noticed how all the actual labor was being accomplished through the will of this central being, Queen, ruler, purpose provider, reality ruler, your highness. We will later learn that this being is called "Sparkle" the Realium Queen.

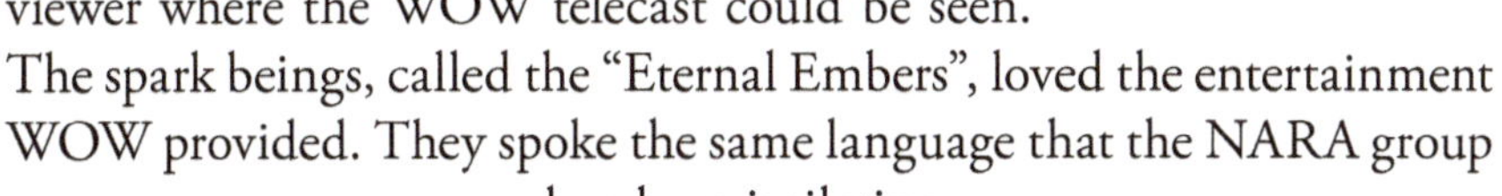

The origins of Realiun are explored in the NARA three recap. NARA two noticed a central viewer where the WOW telecast could be seen. The spark beings, called the "Eternal Embers", loved the entertainment WOW provided. They spoke the same language that the NARA group was already assimilating.

* NARA three started his mission playing favorite tunes on its broadcaster. NARA three would soon be joined by a wispy breezy pixie like being that NARA later called Gusty. Gusty went unnoticed at first but NARA soon noticed the rhythm of the wind burst matched the beat of the music.

Gusty guided NARA three to a small lake, around the lake were one miracle after another. First off was the images NARA three started receiving while approaching the large pond, large pond, or small lake, why the distinction? The answer would soon become clear.

Living flower plants walking around independent of the ground that feeds them. Water beings that greeted NARA three while being flooded with images. In an instant NARA witnessed the billion-year creation of the planet now called Mockery. The central sun with the three orbiting planet sized moons attracted but also repelled any matter that is anywhere close to this contained solar system. The beginning of the inside crust of Mockery is when that massive asteroid lettered with Realium, water, and rock got caught in the pickled gravity field.

The asteroid broke off with sparks as it approached the gravitational field of what was becoming Mockery. After millions of years of shifting the pond finally found a resting place as Mockery continued growing pulling anything towards it. The pond water that was surrounded by Realiun for so long had conscious memory of it the trip through space and the settling as part of a greater being called Planet Mockery.

Pondering its new fate of stagnation within the confines of the natural surroundings, the consciousness of the pond water created hard water constructs. The first water construct is called "Flow," the construct is form from the memory of beings that once explored the asteroid while traveling through space.

Flow became the first of many Ponderer constructs to be born from the pond. Flow could move about where the pond was stuck in one location. Even though the link between the pond and Flow could not be broken, Flow soon developed individuality, realizing the separateness of the oneness.

The images concluded with Flow greeting the NARA probe like they are old friends. Flow is now thousands of years old. Time is measured differently here in Mockery. All this information just streamed through the NARA data base.

It only takes a bit of moisture on sensors for the Ponderer to communicate but Flow finally spoke; **I like what you call music, the wind you call Gusty is always with us, no matter where he is. Gusty is part of the pond consciousness that was created when entering the gravitational field of the central sun As/is. Part of the steam created from entry, Gusty, along with the**

"Eternal Embers" have been here since the beginning of the new cycle.

Now that we can talk, you may find me a little chatty, talking is a slow way of conversing; Flow continued, **talking is the least intrusive form of communication. Seriously, we know all about you, you have touched the consciousness of a cosmic being, and I am being modest.**

The spicket was now a steady trickle as Flow poured out conscious verbal liquidity; Flow informed NARA that the Pond is sending Flow with the NARA unit; **get used to my ponderings. My mate "Tap" is also coming with you, do not worry "Tap" is closed most of the time, you must open Tap up to get anything out of him.**

We have a connection with everything and there is a bond to it all. The Pond is indirectly responsible for you and your crew's arrival, yes, we know about your arrival. Maybe the Flow needs to stop for a while? Just like you NARA, Flow is unintentionally intrusive. You may find me a little bit freaky, but look at yourself, a little flying information gathering robot toy.

Do not fear, go with the flow, smile, we love you.

Flow and Tap wend back to the Gateway shuttle with NARA three, and whether we like it or not, the Ponderers are now part of our crew. You cannot uncrack an egg.

* NARA four came across a small city, what is strange about this city is the lack of roads. No roads or even beaten paths leading in or out of this city. There are no cars, trains, planes, bikes, billboards, or other ordinary things seen on an Earth city. How do the beings come and go?

Fruit trees were all around the buildings with the locals reaping the nourishing fruits. There is a central building that seems to have the most activity, in stealth mode NARA four entered the building that was like a train station, but there were no trains arriving or departing.

Instead, there was row after row of clear tubes with exit doors. The beings would appear, one at a time, inside one of the tubes, exit to go about their business. These beings are more advanced than we first realized, or so it seems.

Was teleportation possibly an ability of these beings? Could the tubes serve an alternative purpose? It appears to be a natural instinctive common way of travel to these little beings. The biggest native we have seen so far are no taller than two feet. Squatty bodies, pointy ears, friendly faces, they were everywhere in the city, walking around purposely with friendly greeting along their way. What that purpose is stands as a mystery, the other mystery is, how was this city got built?

At this point it seemed that their teleportation technology may have some answers as to how we ended in this planet Mockery. This is such a humongous planet and we have only seen a tiny bit of it.

*NARA five did not return at this time, this story will have to wait.

With an up to date summery of the NARA probes adventures, after meeting Flow and Tap, it was time for the crew to explore as well. Zero and Peep may fit in easily, everyone else are giants on/in this world.

Seth shape shifted into a bug to fit in. Zero, Peep and Seth/bug and NARA one decided to visit WOW first. Flow offered, almost insisted to accompany them but gracefully backed down when encouraged to stay.

Zero lets Flow know; **this is just a reconnaissance mission, observe only, introductions are for a later mission. We need to find the best way to conquer this planet, ha, ha, ha.**

Flow responds, **sarcasm, you are a funny being, Zero, I feel your heart and know your true intent, so I laugh with you, ha, ha, ha. I do not have to be with you to be with you, ha, ha, ha. I love you guys already.**

You are all linked like the Ponderers, forever a part of a cosmic Pond consciousness, get used to it. Ha, ha!!

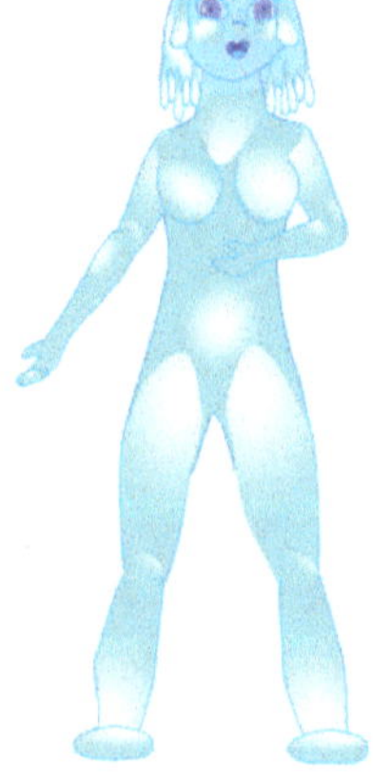

With a scolding chirp, Peep speaks up; **Zero you need to watch what you say, not everyone is as empathic as our new friends Flow and Tap.**

I get what you are saying, Zero responds; **but I know you snickered a little when I said it. World domination has always been my goal, my inner world is in rebellion continually. I am too lazy to conquer, then rule anyone, you know that. Lighten up, bro.**

WOW, HOW and WHY are discussing the metallic object that was seen coming out of the infernal gorge, NARA one translates for the team; **they know something arrived at their enclosed reality in response to their receptive broadcast. The broadcast was about being receptive to any consciousness other than the closed reality of Mockery. A world-wide intention experiments.**

NARA, one agrees to be the bridge to meet these beings, purposefully getting found by a reptile looking house pet. The lizard pup brought it prize catch right to WOW, looking for a treat in return. NARA one reporting; **I am in possession.**

The team returned to the shuttle.

3

ENGAGING THE QUASAVERSE

Reflecting worlds

Back on the Star Ship Neuron, the search party was hard at work. Albert with guidance from Mary has been exploring the galaxy on vision journeys or remote viewing. It is a big galaxy, and we do not know where they are in the timestream.

The Akashic library is being searched for any record of this vanishing event. The Gateway ship logs are being reviewed. Clipper's log is most enlightening. He has a couple theories on the Quasaverse, one theory is essence bubble universes, where the mastery of an essence, 'say music',

has a bubble that all musicians and music end up in that bubble universe. This allows for the Akashic records to be filed correctly. Maybe the Gateway shuttle is in a separate reality, an essence reality?

Another theory from the clipper log journal is consciousness waves, all the consciousness everywhere is like one big ocean, wave/vibration/frequency after wave wash over everything, the waves are guided by intention and observation. Intentions attract similar intentions. Reality can be influenced with the speed of thought, creating a variation stream.

These theories and many more, raised more questions that provided any answers. With no real progress to report at this point only continual due diligence is the obvious path.

 Back on Mockery the crew, with the help of Flow and Tap, started learning the native language. They got fluent very fast; it seems that our elemental friends have telepathic abilities beyond what was first recognized. They get entangled with the water we are all made of, we become part of the pond consciousness in a limited way. The pond is continually expanding its awareness through everything they connect with.

The Ponderers Flow and Tap have the billion-year shared memory that is pond consciousness. Becoming part of this cosmic being is not consensual yet it may be beneficial.

Flow is the first water construct of the pondering pond, even with a shared consciousness, Flow has managed to recognize her individuality. Her sovereignty was recognized as a part of the whole. Tap was right behind flow as the pond wanted to expand its' consciousness. Many constructs (ponderers) were created by the pond. Flow and Tap were chosen to experience from out worldly view-points, chosen for the mission with the Gateway, part of the crew after a while.

Having Flow and Tap around is a bit uneasy. They are beings of both hard and soft water, with all the properties of water; with exception, they do not need a vessel, or, the hard water is hard enough to form their own vessel. They are liquid shape shifters with preferred forms. They hold memory all the way back to creation, memory of every shape they have ever seen.

The Pond communicates with the liquid in other beings, a form of telepathy, they cannot turn it off, so if you are anywhere near them, you are an open book, they know all about you.

The Ponderers are made of ninety nine percent water and one percent Realium. They are immortal and virtually indestructible, yet quite likeable after a while. They are observers, no judgement, innocent in ways, whatever will be, will be. Go with the flow kind of beings.

It is said that there is conscious pond water throughout the universe with an abundance on Mockery. Even the pond owes its being to the element Realium.

Flow insists that the Gateway crew needs Realium to return to familiar home worlds. The best way to get Realium is through Queen Sparkle.

Queen Sparkle does all the dealing for this valuable mineral, the question is, what does the crew have to bargain with? What holds value to beings who help create realities?

Mining Realium

Now we get into the "con" words. Again, it is done in steps. Mining Realium is a long process. Here is the short version: Consciousness, concept/conception, converge, connect, confirm, conform, confide, contain, congregate, consent, consign, confirm, confirm, confirm. Confident conclusion.

Processing Realium

Short version: condition, conscript, confine, condense, condone, convince, conquer.

Crystalizing Realium

Short version: conformist, conformity, conjure, conscience, contemplate, construct, consequence, conclusion.

In our language; the pre-fix "con" means "mind". It is all about the mind. Crystalizing Realium takes place in the mind. It is not mining, it is minding for Realium.

Zero snickered; **maybe we can get a sample of Realium, then use the Realium to create an illusion of value in a piece of paper. Then we can use the newly valued paper to trade for more Realium. Then we can buy the rest of the world before finding our way home.**

Seth offers his insights; **I know you are being funny, Zero, these beings are not fools. You are partially on to something; value is in the eyes of the beholder. Let Sparkle name the terms of trade. Let us see what a Queen holds as value.**

NARA reports: **we are about to become global celebrities, WOW, HOW and WHY know about our arrival and we have an invitation to be on the next Conceptual Moon Broadcast. Letting NARA one, get captured was genius.**

Seth wonders out loud; **maybe we can get an audience with Queen Sparkle? We need to return home!!**

Shawna sooths Seth, saying; **we will be fine, you know they are looking for us.**

Ya!! Zero exclaims; **and we are about to become a global hit. Peep and I will oversee the unveiling, maybe a song for our host WOW. I promise not to embarrass us. No world conquering puns, I swear.**

Clipper offers; **I will see what value we have to offer this Queen. We have a fully stocked cruise shuttle, including a nice gift shop and shopping mall.**

Shawna says, **I will help Clipper; I am the best judge as to what a Queen may like.**

Jinn whispers to himself; **I will hang out in the background and do nothing.**

The crew invited WOW to visit the Gateway shuttle, what they did not expect was WOW suddenly appearing on the bridge where they were meeting. The first thing WOW says is; **this is my spot; we need a clear tube to capture my spot on your ship.**

As WOW greets his host on the Gateway he continues; **You do not want to be standing on my spot if I ever port in again, so capture my spot. Wow!!! This place is amazing, you people are huge, wow!!!**

Flow and Tap are on your ship, wow, who are the rest of you and what is your story.

Zero steps forward; **I am King Zero, king of nothing, you may call me Zero. We are from a planet called Earth. We would be honored to greet your world at your conceptual moon broadcast.**

Peep lands next to Zero saying; **They call me Peep,**

We are happy to greet you. Thank you for receiving us, your world "Mockery" is a micro cosmism of the vast universe. You must already know this and that is why we are here, somehow you brought us here, is one of our theories.

Clipper speaks up; **greetings Sir WOW, as the science officer we need to know the importance of your "spot."**

WOW; it was a great risk to port on your ship without a designated spot, imagine if someone was in that spot that I ported to. We need complete solitude on our spots, even Gusty, a wind elemental, can be harmed just by being in the wrong spot. I can share my spot at timed intervals, every sixty concepts, another port can occur, once a spot is designated.

This explains the port tubes NARA saw in the city; *Clipper replies;* **the tubes are safety devices. I know some of us are giants on this world, we are all gentle beings. Your world should be reassured that our stature has nothing to do with our character.**

Zero interrupts; **no need to explain your lankiness, Clipper, just be careful not to step on anyone. Forgive us in advance for any acts of clumsiness.**

WOW returns to his broadcasting center as the Gateway prepared for this planetary disclosure. They hope it will go smoothly. We are just beginning to see just how vast Mockery is as we review all we know so far.

We are about to become global news here in Mockery. The next broadcast is when the Moon Arrult is directly above. You can watch its approach just by looking up, or in. We have about twenty seven hours towards full Moons Night broadcast.

We are recalling our captured NARA nugget. With that data we can best make our disclosure preporations.

**The Arrult Moon Night
Tell our view-sion Broadcast**

No one on Mockery has ever seen anything outside the womb. There exist a wide diversity of life within the all caring womb. What lyes beyond Mockery's womb has never even been questioned. Until now that is!

Welcome to our conceptual moon broadcast. As you may recall our last broadcast we did a planetary calling to anything beyond Mockery. The ponder-ers have always told stories of infinite existence just beyond our limited perception.

The proof of these stories has answered our call. A wingless shining object spiting energy carried beings here from outside the boundaries of our world and our imaginations. WOW!!! Can you see this, this,... WOW!

Our friend Gecco found this in the courtyard of the gardens. It was placed in our possession to learn our speach.

WOW!! Just one concept ago we had little evidence of expanded reality. What will our next concept cycle reveal?

The Ponder-ers Flow and Tap have met the strangers and walk with them. The Eternal Embers have already started negotiations for Crystalized Realium. Wow!! They make friends easily.

I agree with WOW, I mean WOW! We also have to ask HOW? Did our call bring them, HOW would that work? I feel baffled, stifled and wondered.

This Conceptual Moon broadcast has surprise guest form who knows where. First, we hear from WHY.

This is WHY here! That is a good question, WHY here? I mean WHY Mockery? WHY do we live inside a really large bubble? Enough WHY-ning for now. You may ask yourself, WHY, after viewing what is shared this Moon Night.
Introducing a balance of vibrations, sounds with rhythm our out of world visitors call music.
We bring you!!! What lyes beyond, "The Gateway Band".

The Gateway band plays this catchy ditty to catch the hearts of a world.

As he walked down by the pond,
he started to wonder
what lyes beyond?
Beyond our senses,
over the edge of the shelves,
just past the fences
that we build ourselves.

WOW, it is amazing,
HOW, will we deal,
WHY, should we ponder
what we don't know is real?

Well here we are now,
facing our fears,
relearning the things we thought
we knew all these years.

WOW, it is amazing,
HOW, will we deal,
WHY, should we ponder
what we don't know is real?

The questions on the table,
with our intention being quite pure,
will bring us some answers,
of this we can be sure.

From beyond the beyond
and who knows where,
came a band of strangers
with answers to spare.

WOW, it is amazing,
HOW, will we deal,
WHY, should we ponder
what we don't know is real?

We mastered this,
they love us!

With all of the answers
more questions arise,
there is more to beyond
than we can surmise.

The whole world of Mockery would soon know they are not alone. The effects of this discovery could have some repercussions, nothing would ever be the same.

Queen Sparkle was now aware of the outworlders, the need for Realium is obvious.

We are all quite fluent in the native dialect now so bargaining banter is a welcome challenge. With the help of the Ponderer Flow doing memory transfers, to help everyone along, we learned at record paces. We were ready for the broadcast, so we are ready for the Queen.

4

MOTIONS OF THE QUASAVERSE

Worlds beyond

On the Star Ship Neuron, the search party was making small leaps towards locating the vanished Gateway. Masters of motions from the "Motion Mystery Universe City" have discovered a rogue planetoid the size of a small solar system. It is not certain that this has to do with the vanishing, the miniscule evidence does point towards this rogue.

While tracing motion waves that occurred at the same time as the vanishing, one wave, that only lasted thirty seconds, connected the Neuron Star Ship with this rogue planetoid. This momentary thread is the best clue the search team has.

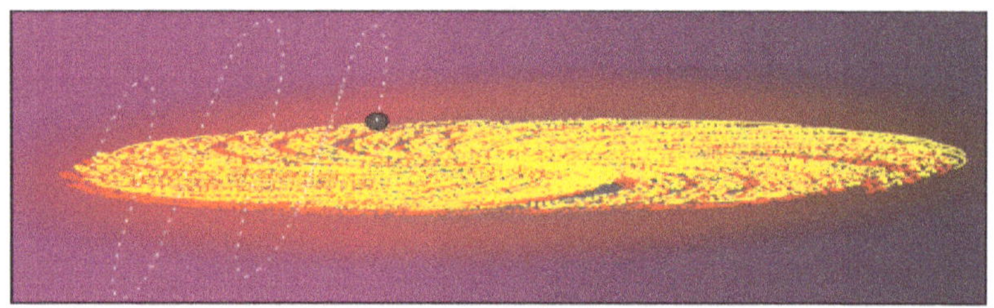

This rogue planet was knocked out of orbit, now weaving in and out the galaxy. Each pass brings mass destruction in the path of this monster.

Could the missing Gateway be in the path? The rogue planetoid is about to collide through the galaxy on another pass. Albert feels the team should do a group dream journey to locate Seth and Shawna. The enmeshment they have is strongest in the dream realm. Making their friends aware of the possible dangers of colliding planets may be all they can do for now.

Myra, with her empathic ability to detect then cure disease, feels the distress coming from the galaxies conscious net within the cosmic taurus field. Galactic illness is much harder to cure, although Myra believes the cure is within reach.

Myra teaches for the Galactic Mystery School, being a Motion Master is a learned ability that helps Myra in her diagnosis as well as healing. Her passions for healing make her the natural leader in the search for the cure.

At the pre dream journey meeting Myra gives a presentation.

Myra; **We have seen how concepts can alter the course of evolution within a civilization, species. Ideas/fictions can be animated to appear real; validation reinforces the illusion; distraction draws you away from the real facts.** **Believing known liars over and over is an illness that is not even recognized. Natural laws are the facts.**

If we operate within natural law, all Mans' laws become irrelevant. We have a long way to go, to even come close to comprehending the fabric of natural law, writing the laws down, teaching the laws are beginning methods towards comprehending them. The laws are fluid with new discovery.

The motions of the universe, the vibrations, harmony, geometry, frequency need to be learned. Using the motions to heal, help and create is good magic, chiseling out new self-centered paradigms is dark magic.

The motions of the universe are energy. A guiding motion is called emotion, stimulating e-motion to a desired response is a tool of manipulation to the selfish students of natural law. Using natural law in the wrong way also has consequences in natural law. Creating fear causes controllable responses; flight, anger, frustration, worry and hopelessness. Emotions are the source of action, reaction.

You may not be familiar with references to the motions of the universe. In the Quasaverse, the motions start with A-motion, E-motion, I-motion, O-motion and U-motion. Then you have co-motion, pro-motion, loco-motion and any other word with the suffix "motion". In the Quasaverse there are many differences, as I am the first being to animate this separate shared reality.

Mastering the motions of the universe (taught in the Galactic Mystery Schools) **starts you on a journey of evolution. OK!! I am plugging another reality. My inner-sane world of image-i-nation.**

A-motion; is the alpha of the motions, one must be master of all the motions to reach A-motion. We are all familiar with E-motion and this motion will be the hardest to continually master.

I-motion is the motion of self, there is a balance one must see to make I-motion aligning with who the "self" includes. O-motion is "one motion" or the recognition of the oneness. U-motion is the motion of everything/everyone around you, it is also looking at other perspectives of I-motion. In a swarm you must be aware of the motion of ones closest to you,

The e-motion of love has the most beneficial frequency to align with the total vibration of the universe. This motion of love is the answer to all life's challenges.

We will be tapping the energy of motion on our discovery dream journey, but to do that, we must first link minds, a task that only Mary, our telepath, can accomplish.

Before was go on the dream journey with the search team we need to return to Mockery.

Queen Sparkle, the royal monarch for the Eternal Embers, Realium realter, sovereign, the realm reigning ruler, brought her best game to the meeting with the Gateway crew.

The arrival of Queen Sparkle along with a full platoon of Eternal Ember guards became a colossal event. Crowds are now gathered around the Gateway landing site, global broadcasting crews from all parts of Mockery are represented at the site.

Realium is Mockery's gold, the most valuable element within the globe. Anything is possible with the proper use of Realium. I have placed Realium on my wand then made it sparkle, you may want this added application. It presents a mystical appearance to your conjuring/con-juring. Remember that "con" means "mind," this, 'mind,' is what really creates reality.

Realium is a catalyst or stepping stone between many realities, your intentions, wishes, and actions are intensified by a tiny bit of Realium. Look at everything around you, all of creation is affected by Realium.

You need to master conjuring to get the true benefit of Realium. First you must outline your wish, express your intent, hold your forearm vertical with your wand at a forty-five-degree angle, rotate three times repeating your intent. Tap the universe with your wand, your results may not be apparent at first. If you do not get any results, you are doing somethings wrong. We deal in quality Realium. Your ability to manifest is determined by your connection with your intent. Clarify your intention and try again, until it works.

It was a dazzling presentation, full of amazing visuals. Queen Sparkles' closing remark was, **value for value, what is your offer?**

Zero steps forward, announcing his imagined royalty, **I am King Zero, King of nothing. You may find this useless to not rule over anything, then again, look at how much nothing there is, 'nothing' is endless. Please, call me Zero, your highness.**

You see what we have. What do you believe to hold value? I can offer you a whole lot of nothing. We can give you the nothing between everything in this planet Mockery, that will make you queen of everything within your nothing realm, all things will be your subjects or invaders within your realm.

As King of nothing, I have the divine right to Grant a small fraction of my vast domain to those that are deserving. You already have the military might of the Eternal Embers to help announce your status change. Do you accept this offer? We will stay for a while, as your guest, of course, to help you create an enlightened society.

The rest of the Gateway crew had to restrain themselves as Zero's offer was never discussed. His logic made sense if you believe in Monarchies, royal blood lines or higher authorities. The task was to not let their anger and surprise show.

Flow sends out a mental remark of caution to the crew, **your clever little friend has poked a nest of what you call hornets. If they even suspect they are being played you will see the**

wrath of Queen Sparkle. You must play along to ensure peace; we will stand with you.

With that being shared among the Gateway crew; Flow speaks out loud to everyone. **What an honor Queen Sparkle, you will rule wisely.**

Having the endorsement of Flow and the Ponderers was what the new reigning queen needed. Sparkle is meant to rule and is now christened High Queen of Mockery by the cosmic visitors. Her reality was manifesting her desired wish and intent.

Zero told the crew, after this was over, that he was under the influence of Sparkles' "Realium" wish and intent, so he was not in his right mind. Although, his status as King of nothing must be recognized, respected, and supported by the crew.

Shawna reminds Zero that we are all Kings and Queens so that makes us all equal. **Sparkle will have to earn our support as reigning sovereign. Now that we have some Realium and a possible way home, we have also assumed a responsibility for our endorsement deal. We need assurance that we made a wise choice in supporting this barbaric paradigm of royalty's rights to rule.**

Queen Sparkle started exercising her authority right after her coronation with a series of royal decrees meant to enforce (with love) the right to rule. Zero became her mentor, his advice was not always in the best interest of the beings they are meant to benefit.

She took to the role/rule like a duck takes to water; **I am Queen Sparkle, your queen, granted queen by the galactic outsiders who have set out to enlighten our planet. My words shall become law, all the queens' decrees must be honored. I am a loving queen that has the full support of the legion of Eternal Embers, who will enforce all decrees. I will rule until such a time when, we can create a system where you can choose your master, based on false promises.**

In Sparkles' rhetoric for the news, she stated; **everyone must conform to**

this newly created monarchy for the rise of Mockery as a galactic player in the outside universe that we are becoming aware of. The crystallization of Realium will back our new ways of living. The Eternal Embers holds all rights to the crystallization process, yet we still need your validations, so keep on reinforcing our rise to becoming power players.

With Zeros' help, Sparkle helped sell a new monetary system to make everyone wealthy, first she had to indoctrinate the concept of what wealth is, (at least her perspective on what wealth is). The new definition of wealth is how much of the new coinage, trade instruments you hold. She also included the illusion of ownership as a means of defining wealth, (in her truth, her crown owned everything).

With the help of How and WHY, spreading the word, broadcasting the coronation then announcing the decrees, change would happen rapidly.

Sparkle, the Eternal Embers, How and Why were promised wealth beyond previously conceived possibilities. The pond and the Ponderers (with no need for wealth) were assured everything was being done for the benefit of the "all being" called Mockery, (the womb mother), the Pond was now "the womb monitor."

At first all the changes in lifestyles were offered as a choice one could make. Sparkle was being tutored by King Zero on how to create a panopticon, a system where those that accept the changes without question would start off ridiculing the non-acceptors, belittlement, a little name calling and eventually even turning the non-acceptors over to the new governing powers that be, (the Eternal Ember police "policy" enforcers).

Create surveillance by convincing others to do the surveillance for you, using whatever methods available. Educate/indoctrinate at young ages, only teach what you want others to learn. Mystify, categorize, demonize, criticize, ostracize, shun, and exclude concepts not in alignment with royal decrees.

Get the populace to turn on each other, through a process of staged events. Divide everyone in as many ways as you can come up with, by status, by beliefs, size, color, and consistence. Claim to be the great uniter. Take advantage of every staged or natural misfortune by claiming to be/have the answer to the dilemmas.

Claim salvage rights for every vessel lost, abandoned, in need of tow or assistance. Become the beacon, the lighthouse, the lead vessel that guides through safe waters. Everyone being towed must go in the direction you take them. You are here to assist, to guide and point towards the safety you are providing. Herding the masses is a shepherds' purpose, use barking dogs to bring any strays back on your desired path. All vessel beings that are not on the path are considered lost or abandoned.

The advice that King Zero was teaching Queen Sparkle, all seem to be methods of capture and imprisonment, being sold as safety and protection. Zeros' lessons of "order from chaos" are only available to select beings with certain self-proclaimed superior energy, beings like Sparkle. The ordained royals all answered to Sparkle and will be sent to different areas of Mockery as regional governors.

It is better to have the populace turning against each other than coming after the crown.

Peep cautioned Zero about revealing tyrannical tactics to a want to be dictator. Peep brought his concerns to the Gateway crew and the Ponderers Flow and Tap. Flow saw the order that seemed to be created by this new concept of government, not realizing the harm a top-down system could have. The Ponderers support for Queen Sparkle was unwavering.

Within a short period of time, Mockery was changed forever.

5

THE SPACE BETWEEN PARTICLES

Dream on

While Mockery was quickly changing, the search team back on the Star Ship Neuron prepared for the dream search journey. They met in the auditorium where all the recording equipment necessary to transcribe the journey was available.

The team telepath, 'Mary,' was the link that makes this shared dream journey possible. Albert, the time/space master, will open the cosmic dream topography displaying the Milky Way Galaxy in now time detail.

The main goal/intent is to locate the Gateway shuttle crew, it is also to determine what can be done, if anything, with the rouge planetoid cascading through the galaxy. If we see what will be affected by the planets' pass, we may also find where our vanished crew is.

Technology allows for the recording of our journey; it is even easier than the dream journal technology. We do not need to sleep; deep meditation will bring us to the dream realm.

With the preparations complete Albert, Mary, Myra, Brandon, Penny, and Charles met up after reaching the Delta consciousness state.

This team reaches the higher states of consciousness easily, the children have less baggage to overcome so they are naturals. From a galactic

view the rouge planet looked like a cue ball on a three-dimensional billiard table. Bill stayed behind as anchor for the team.

As we approached the target area the enormous size of this planet became apparent. It would take a gigantic star to pull this rouge cue ball into a sustainable orbit, the trajectory of this giant would have to be precise to capture it into any order. The geometry is mind boggling,

Following the present trajectory, the potential collisions are numerous. The first possible victim is a small blue marble that looks like Earth. The team visited the planet, they felt the distress of impending disaster coming from the conscious being seeing the approaching gigantic cue ball. The gravitational pull was already causing havoc. There was no sign of the missing crew, something needs to be done, but they must move on.

Nothing could be done as astral projections, the planet has about six months before reaching the point of mass destruction, and the impending collision will hardly alter the course of the giant planet. The cone of probabilities is enormous the further into the timeline you go.

Mary felt a brief connection with Seth and Shawna when they got close to the monster planet, it was so brief she shrugged it off as a passing thought. There was a tremendous amount of psychic energy coming from the planet and it was almost unbearable for such powerful empaths as Mary and Myra. The gut feeling that they are on the right track is stronger than ever.

The overwhelming psychic energy took a lot out of the search crew, they agreed to return to the physical realm, a follow up journey is a must. The data that was acquired was sufficient for now. There was so much at stake. They spotted a massive star in the potential path of the gigantic rouge. Could this be a solution?

As the team revised back on the Neuron, they immediately analyzed the experience they just had. NARAs' main drive computer duplicated a three-dimensional hologram of the Milky Way Galaxy based on what the team witnessed. NARA ran thousands of possible scenarios for the gigantic rouge planet now called "the cue ball."

The next big problem (needing a solution) was our ability to affect the situation, current knowledge is not up for the task, we must dive deeper into the unknown.

Myra was the first to speak up after returning to the physical realm; **I know we all felt the psychic energy coming from the cue ball. Is it possible for anything to survive on that monster? Yet the intensity was almost unbearable.**

Albert responds with his theory; **I felt and saw the history of this cue ball. It has been bombarded by everything in its path, getting larger, for billions of years, like a snow ball that builds up rolling down a snowy hill. It was in the outskirt of the galaxy, acting like a shield, blocking foreign objects from entering the galaxy in that location. A pulse wave from a nearby exploding quasar, knocked it into this erratic destructive path that it has been on for millennia. If there is life on the cue ball it has gone through many mass extinction events in the lifetime of "Cue."**

Cue is set to wipe out that small planet. What do we do about that, Dad? Charles was deeply concerned about the impact of this collision; **the devastation is disturbing.**

There is very little time to figure that out, Charles; there are answers, even if we do not know what they are. The Universe provides.

As the search team continued digesting the new data from the dream journey, back in Mockery word of Queen Sparkle spread throughout.

The realm of nothing had a lot of trespassers, intruding into the nothing. The newly ordained Queen of that nothing is kind enough to not only allow this trespass but welcome the violators under the umbrella that the realm provides. It is the grace of your queen that allows for your very lives. Be grateful to your Queen.

Seth and Shawna briefly felt the presence of Albert and the search team. Shawna got excited as the glimmer of hope quickly want away; **we need a beacon, light a fire, somehow get their attention if they get close again. Maybe we can somehow use this Realium we have purchased using the future of the world. We must stop this path of madness inside Mockery and devise a method to contact the search team we saw in our brief vision.**

The cost of our agreed support for Queen Sparkle is much higher than we thought; Seth replied. **At this point we must play the hand we created. Your idea of some kind of beacon is what we need to do. Maybe we can send out a virtual message in a bottle, into the sea of space.**

We should make a continually repeating message directed out the opening we traveled through; Clipper offered. **This is within our means without using any Realium.**

Maybe we should do a dream journey of our own; Shawna asks? **I am sure they are doing dream journeys searching for us. We are entangled with the search team spirit group. This should happen soon, Realium will help in this quest. The situation here in Mockery with Queen Sparkle must continue with caution, if we show our hand, it would cause havoc. We can fix this with love, that is the only way.**

Jinn hung out in the background doing and saying nothing. He believes that the less he does the less response-ability he will have, yet he was the one who encouraged the cosmic tele-call that got them into this situation. He believes he has proximity magic; miracles happen around him continuously without his effort, if he does less, his proximity magic does less. He never knows the results of his magic. He is the only one that believes he has this ability.

Jinn was standing next to Zero when he spoke up to Queen Sparkle, granting her Queen of nothing in Mockery, this was further evidence to Jinn of his proximity magic. He thinks to himself; just keep out of it, do nothing, know nothing, say nothing.

Is Sparkle queen of my lack of action, my doing nothing? Jinn ponders. I rule over my nothing. Chuckling to himself; even nothing is something, my nothing is acquiescence. Que sara, sara, whatever will be, will be.

It took Clipper a couple days to set up a transmitter at the mouth of the planet opening. NARA sent booster bots throughout the tunnel leading out with a large booster on the outer rim of the opening. A simple SOS message was sent out continuously.

Seth, Shawna, Peep, Flow and Tap discussed the plan for a dream journey. Flow and Tap are already linked telepathically with the crew, as well as everything with water, even the moisture on NARA sensors, this would help in recording the dream journey.

The Ponderers do not sleep or dream, sharing the dreams of the crew will be a new experience for Flow, Tap, and the Pond. They have some experience with dream of the native inhabitants, although these dreams are not lucid controlled experiences. The Pond consciousness is continually impressed with the connection to source creation these galactic visitors have. The new con-cepts the visitors offer appear to be benevolent with a twist of levity. The results of these new concepts are yet to be witnessed.

The Pond consciousness is billions of years in existence, yet seeks knowledge like a beginner. Spreading Pond awareness was the main intension of the Pond. To know the Ponderers you must give up or more specifically share your individuality with them, becoming a Ponderer yourself. In a way, everything in Mockery is part of the Pond consciousness.

Sparkle is Queen of Mockery, Mockery is made of the Pond, the Pond is entangled with everything in Mockery, even Sparkle. Only the Eternal Embers consciousness is separate from the Ponds entanglement.

Flow shared; **Mockery is not the only planet with Pond consciousness, there is another. While the Pond was traveling as an asteroid before crashing into Mockery, a piece of the asteroid with Realium and Pond water broke away in another direction. Based on the visitor's memory of where they are from, the splintered Realium and Pond consciousness are close to Earth.**

Locating the splintered Pond Consciousness will complete the entanglement connection between the crew and the search team.

Giving Albert the location of the splintered Pond consciousness is a main intent of the planned dream journey.

The splintered asteroid collided into the barren moon near Titan orbiting Saturn in the 'Sol' solar system. Organic life on this Titan was/ is nonexistence, this would be a rescue mission for the stranded Pond consciousness and a chance for your comrades to mine some Realium.

This information will be part of our successful soul/spirit connection with you friends back at your home. It will be up to your friend Albert to complete the entanglement.

The dream journey also revealed the massive changes Mockery was realizing, Mockery's society was being affected by contact with the Gateway crew. King Zero was the main catalyst for this change.

Zero formed an inner circle of beings that are loyal to Queen Sparkle. This would open the first class that will become known as "University of the Quasaverse." Professor King Zero lessons are recorded for future classes.

Zero was not an evil, self-centered being, he used due consideration when outlining the concepts that they eventually sold to the inhabitants of Mockery. To sell the new concepts, many events were staged to activate the desired E-motion necessary to create the need. Staging events with the help of mass media made the task easier. You cannot sell protection to someone who does not believe they are in danger. You must form an army to do the protecting, this is done by distributing the land you claimed as rewards/payment for the loyalty.

It is starting to sound like Zero may be a bit evil, diabolical, manipulative after all. He does it all with such good intent and a lovable demeaner. His ideas usually start out as sarcasm, when the sarcasm is taken literally, things take on a life of their own. Just little nudges in the right direction, keeping the main intent in focus and on the target.

Zero, along with the crew of the Gateway, became the power behind the curtain. The authors of a new story, Zero, was the Benjamin Franklin (the go between, the first post master) re-presenting the crew.

Looking at the fantasies that are based almost purely on belief, validation, consent, acquiescence, acceptance; the monetary system is one of the best examples of belief-based reality. The psychic, cerebral, mind control needed to pull this one off is mind boggling. Forget about the support mechanisms such as laws, courts, governments, banks, jails, police, politics, records keeping, education systems and markets. Just look at the deal behind the deal.

The way we become wealthy is to make the beings of Mockery commodities, everyone with consciousness held a value, (even if that value was crystalizing Realium into existence). They all have a present value along with a future value. The plan was to capture that present and future value, to spend it in the now. That value was/is the sweat equity, the creativity, the productivity, the services performed in the existence of a registered being.

What is the deal then? The crown should inventory the populace of Mockery with a mass registration. Each registration will have the value of that beings' entire life span. (Kind of like birth certificates). Each registration is a bond (bondage). The registration is monetized with a small portion returned to the being (usually enough to survive). In exchange, the crew of the Gateway will create a system of exchange using paper notes and coinage, they will create the system of tracking, they will determine who gets what and why.

The crown convinced the Pond, with all the ponderer constructs to monitor the new system, convincing the Pond it was part of a greater creation. The Ponds memory was unlimited, the constructs were everywhere, a perfect record keeping system was already existing. A massive news network was available, the pieces were just falling into place.

The deal with Sparkle and the Eternal Embers to obtain Realium (an element the crew felt they needed to return to their reality) started this whole ball rolling. The Eternal Embers would be useful in staging fear strategies, enforcement rules and crystalizing even more Realium.

As Zero would say; "we are just playing the cards that are dealt to us." The complexities of the deals within the deals get very interesting as you look at who makes out the most in these dealings.

Once the populace inventory is commenced, there can be grants issued for businesses and projects, this will create debt money drawn from the future equity of the registered, the promise to pay, the present and future value, all are the collateral to get the ball rolling. You will be able to finance your way out of this planet to become part of a cosmic society.

Some of these issued grants will be used to back and create a central banking system that will be given the printing press, further indebting the registered creditors. Hire the bankers to do your job (the crown), make money out of nothing then charge interest. Use other beings' credit to finance their debt slavery. Create confusion as to how the system works.

Create branch banks that loan out currency using a fractional reserve system, allowing the branches to create currencies out of nothing (the credit of the registered) give out "loans" to the creditors, charge interest on this newly created bank asset. For the use of credit, making the crew wealthy, offer to pay all accrued debts of the creditors but make it an impossible task, so that only one in a billion will figure it out. Only the inner circle will have this advantage of debt discharging.

In this way, everything will be pre-paid, yet you can still make the creditors pay even more. Attach a precious metal or mineral, such as Realium, to the system that gives the illusion of value. Claim to have possession of large amounts of these metals or minerals in a locked vault that no-one can open and look inside.

This process will eventually move your planet into a higher state of being, the capturing will show the need for freedom to the wisest among you. This desire for freedom will open a consciousness level needed to advance closer to source.

What role did Jinn play in setting up this capture of an entire planets most valued energy, (its' inhabitants)? He is magical but he does not do magic, Jinn would rather sit back and do nothing, yet magic happens around him, a magic magnet.

Miracle after subtle miracle happen continuously. The trick is spotting the miracle then using it to build on reality. There were so many factors contributing to the vanishing of the Gateway space shuttle and the appearance inside Mockery; eventually Jinn's' miracle magic proximity ability was looked at quite closely, at first Jinn kept his suspected ability to himself. Jinn is a back-seat player that effects everything.

The capturing of the beings of Mockery could not have happened without Jinn. Being a being of pure belief, a manifestation, a fiction brought into existence, or someone who assumed the role of Jinn when the need arrived; he was still the miracle man. The way everything just fell into place inside Mockery was a miracle on its own.

To expand the registration of the populace along with the territory of the captured planet, a survey was needed that would lay out a grid of everywhere in Mockery. Luckily that grid map already existed in the halls of the scholars. Assigning each grid, a zip code number, was a way of keeping track of the conquered/captive planet, the great registration sounds better. Shhhh! The beings of Mockery do not know they are being conquered.

While Jinn sat back and did nothing, a whole planet was hoodwinked by his fellow crew members. Even Flow and Tap, who also just went along with everything, never felt like conquerors. Conquering was never the up-front intent, or even a passing thought to anyone yet the inevitable outcome of their actions was known by a few.

Both Seth and Shawna (the pilot and captain, of the Gateway craft), have experience in multiple timelines, yet they chose this path of opportunity to keep peace, over common-sense decency. They are well schooled in the laws of cause and effect, the motions of the universe, and natural law, yet little was done at first to stem the wave of negative change in Mockery.

We are getting ahead of ourselves, the twist this story takes has many consequences, it is best to keep to a linear timeline while recapitulating this story adventure.

The dream crew met on the bridge of the Gateway shuttle to begin the dream journey. Flow was the connection but was just along for the ride. Seeing the universe from outside of Mockery for the first time in millennia was like walking out into the sun after being in a cave for a long time. Even the splintered Pond fragment on Titans moon view of the cosmos was blocked by clouded atmosphere of metallic particles.

In the dream landscape they could travel with the speed of thought. The advantage this team of dream travelers has is they know where they are going, they know where the Star Ship Neuron is, next stop is Albert's search team.

With Flows' help the transfer of information into Albert's dream was almost instantaneous. Flow was also able to view the events of Albert's search team. Could Mockery be the Cue Ball they are worried about?

The revelations from this journey gave new directions for both ends of the spectrum of the story.

6

BRIDGING THE COSMOS

Common Goals

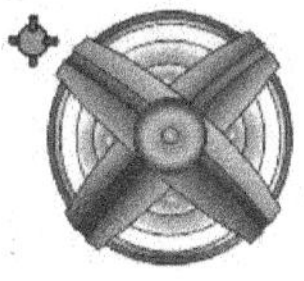

When Albert woke up after a sound restful slumber with the excitement of a little boy that finds a marble. Mary shared his excitement even without their psychic link. They gathered the search team to share the dream revelations.

After a detailed synopsis of the dream, Albert summarized; **we need to organize a rescue/retrieval of the Splintered Pond consciousness on the nearby moon of Titan, that is orbiting Saturn. We also suspect that the vanished crew of the Gateway Shuttle is inside what we call the "Cue Ball." Seth called the "Cue" "Mockery," this must be the name they call our gigantic rouge planetoid.**

We felt a massive amount of psychic energy coming from Cue on our dream journey; Mary added, **we even felt our connection with Shawna and Seth briefly. The universe seems to be providing what it needs to heal itself, this is all to coincidental.**

Exposing, entangling mankind to a godlike cosmic consciousness like the Pond must be done on a free will basis, Penny notes; **this is a marriage that has no divorce. Once you are**

part of the Pond consciousness you are a Ponderer forever. That is what I see in this plan.

We will have to isolate and limit exposure to the splintered Pond that we rescue, Albert states**; I will be the only contact with the Ponderer, until we know more no one should be exposed. I have already felt the Ponderers influence in my shared dream, there is no reason to risk anyone else.**

NARA started producing NARA mining drones, NARA builder drones, NARA isolation drones with a dehydration shield to protect contamination of unwanted Pond exposure. Somehow, we need to re-unite the splintered Pond with the Ponderers.

NARA's mission intent; retrieve and isolate splintered Pond and mine for Realium, two teams of drones will start out the mission, as we continue replicating, we can split into smaller multitasking. A mining crew of drones will set up a base to continue mining. It will only take small samples of the Pond and Realium for everything to start.

The NARA builder drones will build the isolation ship with fully equipped labs for the samples retrieved. This isolation ship must be a distance from Neuron or any populated space port.

Within two weeks a personal shuttle was set out for the Titan moon with Albert and the NARA mining drones. It is a forty-eight-hour space trip, not much to look at so Albert kept busy preparing for his walk on a moon that man has never explored.

The visitation dreams informed Albert the exact location of the Splintered asteroid on the moon. The Pond never lost contact with the splintered asteroid Pond, the consciousness entanglement cannot be severed by time, distance, or matter.

After landing on the Titan moon near the asteroid crash site, Albert wasted no time getting into his space suit and heading out on his quest to rescue the splintered Ponderer and retrieve a sample of Realium.

Before long Albert was joined by a guide from the splintered Pond. The hard water construct calls himself Clog, he leads Albert to a vein if crystal Realium, this quest went without a hitch.

NARA miner and builder drones were left on the Titan moon to complete the rescue mission and retrieve Realium. There was enough metal in the atmosphere of the moon to provide material for NARA replication as well as build living quarters for continued mining.

Clog became Albert's' best friend and constant companion while they stayed in isolation. With Clog around Albert was able to contact the vanished crew of the Gateway at any time. The Ponderers entanglement with Albert was complete. Clogs unconditional love was assuring to Albert, the free will choice to accept the entanglement was necessary at first but now is welcome.

Clog looked like one of Penny's bubble constructs, made solid by Charles, and translated by Brandon, this comparison helped Albert not miss the family as much while in isolation. Clog is a Ponderer with a shared consciousness but also has self-consciousness, aware of individuality. This individuality cannot be given up when entangling with any Ponderer.

This NARA unit (narrating the story) does not completely comprehend the relationship between a vessel 'Ponderer' and the Pond consciousness. The facts point towards a mutually beneficial union, giving the vessel the memory of a cosmic entity, also the ability to remote view, remote experience what other Ponderers anywhere are experiencing (entanglement), and giving the Pond consciousness another perspective of the garden universe expanding cosmic awareness. Most Ponderers continue their lives without even recognizing the entanglement.

Treating the Ponderers like a contagious disease is a caution, we really know nothing except what we are informed by the Pond. Trust but verify is the best course of action. Albert's sacrifice of his family during the quarantine isolation time was made bearable because of the monumental task, keeping busy was the best remedy.

Albert spent half his time in his astral form visiting the stranded Gateway crew inside Mockery.

In the meantime, the Pond with be a direct link with Seth, Shawna, and the crew of the Gateway shuttle, through Flow and Tap, meet Albert's spirit to discuss the best way to stop the galactic calamity of Cue/Mockery impending collisions.

The small blue marble, first target in the path of Cue, is the first concern. Somehow saving the inhabitants is the best solution at this close a proximity. In five months, the collision happens, it will hardly affect Mockery's inhabitants, Mockery will be knocked into a new forward path.

Clipper was the one to come up with the idea for saving the inhabitants of the small blue marble. **WOW and his fellow beings are all teleporters, have you ever tested the limits of your ability?** Clipper continued asking WOW a series of questions; **is our presence here in Mockery a result of this teleportation ability? Now far can you teleport? Can you teleport with someone or something great distance?**

WOW is quickly becoming a member of the Gateway crew; his continual coverage of the visitors is a global hit. The rise into power by Queen Sparkle also helps keep WOW in the number one slot of world broadcasters. This new information that Mockery is a galactic calamity has not been shared yet.

We are not sure if our teleportation ability brought you here; WOW starts out with his best answers. **Just hours before your arrival we had a world broadcast asking questions about existence beyond our limited reality here in Mockery, you are the answer to that question. We have been known to teleport great distance; to answer another question, but never outside the boundaries of Mockery. It may be possible; we do not know.**

Teleporting with someone or something is done all the time, some take their pets wherever they go. How do we test the limits of our ability? For us it is as natural as walking.

Testing your ability comes with risks, teleporting in general has many risks already, that is the reason for designated spots protected by private tubes. Clipper continues; **first you must be able to visualize your destination, that is why you have never left Mockery, you cannot visualize it. You have a designated spot here on the Gateway shuttle, if we go into "outer space" you should be able to visualize and teleport.**

WOW agreed that this may be possible; **if we take the Gateway to the planet, you should still be able to teleport?** WOW shrugs his shoulders in uncertainty. The next step is to test these theories by taking the Gateway to the small blue marble that we need to name. **I suggest we call the planet "Yikes;"** Clipper suggest.

Planet "Yikes," I am sure that is what the inhabitants are thinking right now; Seth speaks up, **this trip needs to happen soon. We also need to see just what is in the path of Mockery. This is why we are here. We take off for Yikes in five-hours. WOW you are welcome to come with us and be the first to leave the womb of Mockery. Flow and Tap are welcome also, the wisdom of the Pond is more than welcome.**

The lift off, of the Gateway went on schedule, the path through the thick crust of Mockery has some challenges they did not encounter on the way in. First off, it took much longer to leave, the magnetic gravitational shifts caused turbulence throughout the shuttle. Seeing the vastness of space when the ship emerged was a Wow for WOW. It was a Wow for the whole crew.

The NARA navigational system mapped everything in the area, the initial scan was quick although continual scans continued the whole journey. The first scan gave them the direction of Yikes.

Just beyond Yike's solar system is a nebula of stars being formed, the star minerals saturate the nebula. Passing through the nebula would incinerate any organic life, Mockery would lose everyone, if we bring the beings of Yikes here, they will be going from the frying pan to the fire.

Even the Pond would cease to exist, only the Eternal Embers would survive. If Mockery strikes Yikes on the front side, it will be knocked directly into the nebula, if it strikes on the back, it will deflect Mockery to safety.

How can we control the path of destruction? Mockery is like a runaway train with no brakes. The plan to save the beings of Yikes, still a work in progress, will proceed even with this new hurdle to overcome.

As the space shuttle Gateway heads to planet Yikes, we turn our attention back to the Queen Sparkle saga inside Mockery. Not everyone in Mockery was accepting the reign of Queen Sparkle. The unrest was peacefully resolved with a global broadcast presented by HOW and WHY.

Queen Sparkle spoke with reassuring grace, her intentions are pure, meant to benefit everyone; **it is important that all beings know of the Trust you have with the Crown. When the crown says Trust, it really means contract. Due consideration is a major characteristic of any contract/trust, this means that the contract must be beneficial to both parties of any contract/trust.**

The beings of Mockery are the whole faith and credit for the realm, everyone is wealthy with a generous Trust account for each subject. You can use this Trust account to improve your life, safety, health, and life style will be improved in ways you may discover on your own.

It has become my destiny to herald and orchestrate Mockery towards a vivacious civilization. This can only be done with the vision of the completed puzzle picture, the blue print for society is being shared by our outer world friends. King Zero's knowledge is the light guiding the way.

What does a vibrant society look like? Mockery is a being, made of all of us, everything, including my realm of nothing, make up Mockery. Visualize a healthy Mockery, a planet that uses

the resources naturally provided to insure the most beneficial results for all.

The crown is producing these coins with the image of your Queen Sparkle. Each of the coins will have

a bit of Realium, giving them value. With these coins you/we can manifest the paradise you/we may vision.

The back of the coin has an image of our cosmic visitor King Zero, the space vessel Gateway, and two of our protecters Eternal Embers. The coins cannot be replicated outside the crown.

One must produce value to earn these coins, the more coins you collect the more you can manifest. The coins hold a value of one token. You may ask, what am I token on? I am on the token, not token on anything.

One out of every ten tokens will be paid back to the Crown, to pay for producing the coins, then operating the exchange system. This tiding will prevent saturation with de-valuing effects, allowing the crown to finance large projects, that are beneficial to all.

With the Pond consciousness tracking, protecting, transferring, banking the currency, everyone will thrive. This is a new way of interacting with each other, the real value is you, the more value you offer the more you will prosper.

Mockery is set to become a stellar galactic player so we must be our best.

Queen Sparkle's global broadcast was seen by most everyone in Mockery. The new coin exchange system was being excepted everywhere. Coin production and distribution was already well underway. The raw materials needed for production was already in place as the Eternal Embers have been mining for thousands of years.

The lesson that Sparkle resonates with is that her role is the big puzzle orchestrator, to bring order on the large scale so everyone can focus on their local puzzle picture. To make existence easy and beneficial, to get society to operate in harmony with our shared reality being created by Realium. This was her role as queen of the Eternal Embers, she is a natural leader.

King Zero is relieved that Sparkle has a wisdom of her own, that she follows the heart center with her own conclusions, a true sovereign. Painting a picture, introducing a concept, teaching, reading, observing are stepping stones and tools on the path to freedom.

Being Sovereign is a continual journey, as the Sovereign gains wisdom they realize that we are all individual parts of one. Love-reigns is the higher step of being Sovereign. Zero looks for the quality of an advanced Sovereign when offering a position with the Collective Crown.

Maybe the Gateway crew can finally help the beings of Mockery, make up for the folly of Zero's momentary intervention (making Sparkle Queen of Mockery). This action mushroomed into a full-scale remodeling of an existing society.

7

COSMIC RESOLUTIONS

United efforts

You are familiar with Realium, so you know that Un-Realium must exist also, somewhere in the Quasaverse. Is Un-Realium abundant, everywhere? Is Un-Realium the opposite of Realium, or the absence of Realium, possible the same as Realium? Clipper, obsessed with answering these questions, he rambled on. He also expressed his theories on convergence of multiple realities based on common denominators, common essences, common vibrations.

What do Clipper's theories of Un-Realium have to do with the rescue of Yikes inhabitants or the rampaging planetary cue ball rapidly approaching Yikes? Seth wonders about Clipper's confused theories.

What I suggest, Clipper continued; **is that with Realium we can accomplish what we believe is Un-Realium or impossible. We need to operate on an impossible scale. Everything is falling into place; do you feel that it is just a coincidence that we ported to a planet full of teleporters? That we have the needed vehicle to travel about and recognize the possible result of Mockery's path?**

We are the white blood cells the Galactic consciousness sent to heal the Milky way's illness. We are on a holy mission of cosmic origin. The answers are right in front of us, we just need recognition.

While the crew of the Gateway ponders the next step to take on this rescue mission, let us look at a brief history of Mockery.

What was existence like in Mockery before the arrival of the Gateway ship and crew?

Pre arrival, Mockery had some disputes among the diversified beings, although everyone respected and got along quite nicely. Everything needed for life to thrive is/was abundant. The technology was advanced for a closed society.

The inhabitants took advantage of the central sun with three orbiting moons within the vastness of Mockery's core. The inside crust where most of life resided, was vast beyond imagination, with a variety of natural wonders. The dynamics of this mini solar system inside a celestial planet is something to behold. The outside of Mockery is a barren, crater filled waste land. No one would know that many civilizations existed inside this gigantic ball barreling through the galaxy in an erratic orbit.

With the diversity of beings, each with a special set of needs, it was a natural ecological distribution of resources. Conflicts rarely arose and were easily resolved. The concept of having possessions beyond your needs and wants was not even considered. Can you believe, there has never been any wars in Mockery. No Empires, no conquest, no plantations no need to take more than needed to thrive in living life.

Queen Sparkle is the first Empire builder ever in Mockery. With proper guidance she will unite the beings of Mockery to handle the tasks ahead of them.

Technology is new to Mockery. Inner planet travel along with mass communication are also new to the inhabitants. Only WOW along with his fellow beings (the Poples) had navigated the interior of Mockery. Their teleportation abilities allowed them to go just about anywhere within Mockery. The other beings had limited range and stayed close to where they lived.

The Ponderers did not travel as they are a part of every living thing in Mockery, it is not necessary to travel if a part of you is already there.

As you have probably surmised, the surface of Mockery gets bombarded with collisions quite regularly. The crust is so thick that most impacts are hardly noticed inside Mockery's interior womb. Larger collisions would cause a vibrational wave within the core, the wave vibrations are filtered through the inner caverns of the crust that cause what some call the frequency of life.

The great harm on the outside of Mockery brings pleasure to the inner side of the planet. There must be a better way to ring this enormous bell. Each impact leaves its signature/essence on Mockery, a sort of melding takes place, somehow nothing is completely lost in any collision into Mockery. Many things die and it is a great tragedy, yet something occurs, miracles if you like, to preserve consciousness of each impact.

It is time to bring this chaos into order, somehow the task was coming to light, a truth that everyone could see. WOW is the catalyst that brings the awareness of Mockery's rampage, shocking the beings into disbelief, then ridicule, finally acceptance with determination.

WOW is the hero of this adventure, the risk he took teleporting from the Gateway on the planet Yikes to his safe spot inside Mockery was the solution to saving many of the beings of Yikes.

The mission was clear, the Gateway shuttle will return to Mockery to pick up as many Poples teleporter volunteers as possible then return to Yikes. Each volunteer can save up to ten Yike inhabitants. Once the Poples have a safe visual space on Yikes, they can make several trips. The closer Mockery gets to Yikes the easier the teleportation will be.

Back on the Star Ship Neuron the search team has changed the purpose of the soul group. Albert's Entanglement with the Ponderer Clog connects the crew of the Gateway with the soul team. The search is complete, the new purpose has been revealed.

Albert remained in isolation, he is already a vessel that has touched the infinite, although his connection with space/time is not contagious. Being around the Ponderer Clog or entangling with the Pond is like touching the infinite. Most still think that exposing yourself to a contagious enlightenment that brings cosmic awareness is a risk to free will.

Albert's family and the search team are willing to make the leap, take the risk, choose the entanglement, all to join Albert. The short time spent as a Ponderer has only benefitted Albert so far. Caution is still the guiding path.

Myra, the team healer, agreed with Clipper, the events all point to galactic conscious purposeful intervention. It is an honor to serve cosmic intelligence, she could sense that everything was progressing, manifesting in divine order.

Myra believes that there is a remedy for all dis-ease, no matter how large the illness, it still has a cure. The cure may be death, although that leads to birth. The cycle of life is the natural course of nature, the living prefer life though.

The team agreed that other essence masters are needed on the team to tackle the problems being revealed. Even the greatest sovereign minds recognize the need for specialized mental masters. The world's leading billiard player (Sure Shot MaGee) is recruited to help. Billiards are played on a two-dimensional plane or table, three-dimensional pool is being played on the Star Ship Neuron, the balls are holograms that interact with each other as if solid. Sure Shot has mastered the game like no other.

The holographic billiard room is being modified to resemble the Milky Way galaxy. Backtracking the path of Mockery took a lot of research in the cosmic library (Akashic Records). The shared entanglement of Clog with the Pond helped, the harmonic resonance occurrences throughout the past are all collision events. Timing these events helps calculate the path.

The size and mass of Mockery compared to surrounding objects is a major consideration in setting up the existing scenario. Our Earth is about the size of the planet Yikes. Yikes is the size of a golf ball while Mockery is the size of a large beach ball, this comparison is close to reality.

With all the effort into detail, the best they can do is make a good guess as to what will happen, what they are sure of is, not doing anything is not an option. If Mockery strikes Yikes wrong, they will deflect course enough to head Mockery in the direction of a star forming Nebula that will fry Mockery like a hard-boiled egg.

There are many unanswered questions, somehow the answers to these questions present themselves when needed the most. While the stage was being set in the holographic room, the obvious questions became a priority. The most critical answer needed was how to affect Mockery's path, or even the path of Yikes? The fact that altering a planets path has never been accomplished, is not a deterrent.

The efforts of the researchers do pay off with the possibility of getting Mockery to start orbiting a nearby gas giant big enough to capture such a large planetoid. The Nebula produced then placed this gas giant in the potential path of Mockery, another sign of divine intervention. The universe must be confident that the path of Mockery can be altered.

With the completion of the holographic images, Sure Shot identified the sweet spot, the spot-on Mockery that Yikes needs to strike to adjust the path enough to miss the Nebula and head towards the gas giant. It would take one more shift with precise timing to create the orbiting.

The connection/entanglement between Clog and the Pond allowed for continual communications with the most recent updates. Clog showed Albert the efforts of the Gateway on their rescue (res-cue) mission.

Albert's shares the triumph of the team on Mockery, the rescue (res-cue) of Yikes inhabitants takes a couple turns. This story has elements of challenge, inspiration, wonder and miracles.

8

INTERSTELLAR BILLIARDS

Consequences

The Gateway shuttle is like a large cruise ship capable of housing, transporting one thousand people. The trip between Mockery and Yikes takes about forty-eight hours, that distance is rapidly decreasing. 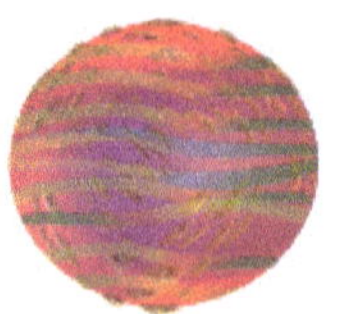

Before leaving Yikes, the crew did some exploring, a chance to meet the beings of Yikes. What they found would enable them to preserve much of Yike's life and culture. The landing of the Gateway shuttle was seen by many, already in a panic mode, the Gateway was taken as another threat. It did not take long before the shuttle was surrounded by thousands of the indigenous beings. They held objects that looked like weapons. the weapons will not even scratch the paint on the shuttle, everyone is safe inside. 

Shawna launched a couple NARA probes to learn what they could, the inhabitants seem to be chanting. The NARA survey showed that the crowd was making way for a small entourage of beings heading towards the Gateway shuttle, this is obviously the leaders coming to confront the crew.

In the center of the entourage was a tall golden fleeced being, dressed in what might be a scientific protective hazmat suit. The outfit could also be ornamental as there was no hood or head gear.

As they approached the leader, who looks like a Lama, is a kind and wise being. Flow has been melding with the locals since we landed, learning the native dialect. Flow was able to mentally greet the leader as he approached.

The gathered inhabitants eased their tension as Flow calmed the energy by announcing the pure intentions of the mistaken invasion. **We are here to help**, Flow assured.

I am the golden patriarch, speaker for the aggregate, lead scientist, here to greet you. I am not the leader, there are no leaders.

Flow shared the big picture with Goldy, then announced the plan, we need a volunteer from your planet to go with WOW as he teleports back to Mockery. This is very risky as it has never been done. If successful we can save a larger percentage of you.

From out of the crowd, Wabble, a brave spirit, came forward, offering to Teleport with WOW. Wabble; **we must do something, take risk, I do not fully comprehend what is needed, but I am ready for anything.**

WOW welcomed Wabble while enticing the crowd to encourage their new hero; **place your positive support and intentions for Wabble, this will help to ensure our success.**

The shuttle will be loaded also, making as many trips as possible before collision. Everyone must remain calm, centered, to make it easier.

Wow took Wabble by his paw. Poof!!! They were gone. The amazement was second to the intensity of anticipation, it would only moments to hear if the teleportation succeeded, it seemed like an eternity. Flow did a happy dance as the Ponderers on Mockery experienced the arrival of WOW with Wabble as they pooped into WOW's safe spot enclosure tube.

Everyone on Yikes cheered, hope and excitement spread like a wave. The Gateway shuttle started loading the natives for the first run back to Mockery.

Back in Mockery.

Up to this point, the beings of Mockery have not been informed about the coming collision or the fate of Mockery. The Ponderers kept the coming disasters quiet, WOW would bring the news to the inner world.

When the Gateway returned to Mockery on their first trip, WOW was ready with hundreds of his fellow beings ready to help with the Yikes rescue.

Zero was on a different mission than his crew mates. He was busy setting up the Crown Collective and mentoring the royal cabinet.

An attempt to introduce the concept of LAW to the Crown, Zero, taught all the variants of Law as well. Most of Mockery already practiced individual law, making community laws unnecessary. If the Crown did nothing about LAW, Mockery would be better off. The full cycle lesson about LAW brings you back to Individual Natural Law. The new LAWs complicated life for most everyone, but greatly benefited a few.

Laws, codes, rules, regulations, Policies, mandates, decrees, requirements, are at best, suggestions. They are also tools for bullying, pirating, capturing, controlling, and limiting, it is up to one's intention as to how LAW is used. Enforcing LAWs is only needed when harm is being committed, do no harm is the first law of the unwritten Natural Individual Law.

There are four branches needed to enforce, or force the law on the unsuspecting community. Policing is only needed for those that cannot police themselves.

Policing is the first branch of the enforcement process; this is a good thing until the law makers want policies enforced that do not bring harm. At some point, without morals, they become revenue agents, policy enforcers, kidnapers, minions.

The next branch is the law-yers, the policy makers, defenders, advocates for the captured spirits, loyal to the Crown. If unchecked they can put you in cages to protect you and protect others from you. The Law-yers take you to a court where they can beat you about with their racket. in front of the next branch of enforcement, Judges, banker, or clergy that determine your fate.

If the court finds you or fine you guilty of defying their statute, they need a way to punish, coerce, reform, to get you to conform. This is where the cages are used.

All these enforcement strategies are needed to replace Self Governing. The peace that was a natural occurrence in Mockery is about to become a peace, that the Crown Collective enforces.

Queen Sparkle used discretion when hearing Zero's lessons in civilization building, may she find the wisdom to separate the jewels from the muck.

Back at the Starship Neuron Albert's soul group witnessed, second hand, the rescue of Yikes. The biggest question being researched is how to deflect Mockery to the desired path, avoiding the star creating Nebula that could fry Mockery. The sweet spot and angles have already been calculated; the orbit of Yikes needs to be slightly altered to strike Mockery just right. What will it take to move a planet?

Albert's family is joining him in isolation. The entanglement with the Ponderers does not appear to cause harm, in fact the mingling with the Pond brings one closer to Source Creation. It is still a large decision, choosing this path cannot infringe on others free choice. This family is used to exploring new realities, this merging with the Pond is another adventure.

Myra will remain behind to monitor from a distance, she will lead the research project from the Star Ship. There is much to do, as the rescue of Yikes continues, the master minds work on the deflection of Mockery. This monumental task needs a solution now. Theories are submitted by the greatest scientist known. The main theory is using an active volcano on Yikes as a booster to blast the planet in the direction needed to alter the path of Mockery. This will only work if the volcano is intensified and implode instead of exploding. The angles and timing are crucial.

9

CUE BALL SIDE POCKET

Submission

Clipper remained on Yikes helping with the evacuation and mapping the planets topography searching for solutions. The golden patriarch of Yikes was a great help bringing all known knowledge to the table. The first piece of information was the real name of planet Yikes, the natives call the planet Ricochet.

Ricochet, like many other planets, has a hollow core with a central sun like Mockery, except on a much smaller scale. Inner Ricochet is not populated like most planets, this will help when a solution is decided upon.

The Gateway shuttle was on the fourth-round trip from Mockery to Ricochet/Yikes, time is running out and they estimate that they can make two more trips before collision. The beings of Ricochet struggled to reach the rescue site, coming from all corners of the planet we have millions of stories. Gravity was chaotic, the solar system sun was getting further away as Ricochet/Yikes is pulled out of orbit by the approaching giant called Mockery.

Earthquakes, tsunamis, massive storms are occurring continually. Many are choosing to go down with the ship, the love for their home was linked, leaving would be like abandoning their family. The cycle of life will continue with a new awareness. A group of those chosen to remain behind have volunteered to help any way they can. The task that these brave souls undertake will save the lives of trillions.

Clipper has been working with Albert through their entanglement with the Ponderers. Flow was critical in helping them master their new entanglement abilities. The existing path of both planets has been calculated, the sweet spot and angle needed to deflect Mockery is known. The plan is to cause the core sun to detonate, blasting Ricochet in the desired path.

The southern pole has a large opening leading to inner Ricochet, the Gateway shuttle placed a rocket at the mouth of the port hole to be launched at just the right moment, causing the implosion of the inner sun, Ricochet/Yikes central singularity, blasting the planet in the desired direction.

The small team of brave indigenous souls will launch the rocket. The sacrifice of this team will have songs written about them, going down as galactic heroes, remembered for all eternity. That is, if the plan works.

Of course the plan will work, this is the universe healing itself. With all the dangers ahead, there is an inner confidence that does not allow for any doubt.

The mass immigration of Ricochet beings into Mockery is causing problems that should be easily solved in this abundant planet. Just recently the populous believed they were the only beings in existence. Now they are seeing new beings invading their limited paradigm, creating fear of the unknown. Calming the fear before it spreads like a wildfire was a convenient tool for the Crown to enforce their newly forming authority inside Mockery.

King Zero has tutored the Crown on designed opposition and controlling the narrative. While fanning the flames of the fear bonfire, the Crown promised to be the solution to the out-of-control chaos. Taking advantage of a disaster to gain power is a tactic used by conquerors through-out time.

The Crown organization **was** very helpful in receiving the added populous, transporting the new arrivals throughout Mockery to keep any one region from being overwhelmed. In fact, the Crown was what Mockery needed at this time of great challenges.

The Gateway shuttle followed the instructions of the Crown when dropping off the refugees from Ricochet/Yikes. Each location was prepped to receive the influx of new beings, sanctuary can only be offered with an open heart/mind and planned integration. It is not sustainable to burden one region with a massive influx, the available resources would not be able to handle the situation.

WOW, HOW and WHY used the planetary broadcasting network to keep the populous informed. Wabble (the first Ricochet/Yikes refugee) is now a household name. WOW, along with hundreds of volunteer Pople teleporters continued teleporting Ricochet/Yikes beings up until the last moments before the now planned actual ricochet of Mockery, saving everyone.

Isolation tubes that allow for safe teleportation were installed to allow for multiple arrivals and departures. Planet to planet teleportation has never been done before, the proximity of the two planets has made the impossible possible. The exhausting toll of multiple teleportation was starting to ware out the Pople heroes. The empathetic desire to help others is innate, tasking your abilities to their limits is pure willpower. Preserving life is accomplished by pre-serving life, then serving life.

Operation Ricochet is what the deflection of Mockery is called, the launch of Ricochet/Yikes was rapidly approaching. Everything is in place; the orchestration of events was being governed by the Starship Neuron. Synchronizing clocks was accomplished through the Ponderer's entanglement network. Countdown in twenty-four hours, last minute preparations are underway. Extraction of the brave launch team is planned although the risks may out way the mission, they are prepared to make the ultimate sacrifice.

Everything was happening at a rapid pace, individual stories would fill up a library, this story is being told from a wide encompassing lens. At times we need to focus the lens on single events or players to tell this story. Zooming in we find the Gateway shuttle making the final round trip to Ricochet/Yikes. The launch of the rocket went smoothly, the Gateway was heading to extract the launch team when the planet shifted or lunged into the new desired direction. Parts of the planet were flying off into space, the shuttle crew held their breath hoping the planet would hold together long enough to strike Mockery. The hard decision was made, the Gateway shuttle departed Ricochet/Yikes.

The Ponderers entanglement link with the launch crew could be felt by everyone as their final moments took place. The emotional range from fear to love, from terror to calm, from birth to death, was experienced by all the Ponderers everywhere. Ripples of emotion trembled across the surface of the Pond; the Pond had never experienced such a tragic yet heroic event in the entire existence.

The Gateway shuttle remained in outer space to monitor operation Ricochet. The integrity of Ricochet thankfully held up as it barreled towards Mockery on the corrected path. Ricochet course was heading straight to the designed sweet spot-on Mockery, so far things were going as planned.

When Ricochet struck Mockery, the vibration echoed throughout the planet. The harmonics created by the caverns are almost hypnotic as the vibration's frequency ebbed and flowed.

At first it the new path of Mockery seemed to miss the Nebula, the calculations showed that the course adjustment was not quite enough, Mockery will still brush the edges of the Nebula. The good news was that there is time to figure out the next step to prevent harm.

Thankfully most of Ricochet inhabitants are now safe inside the womb of Mockery. The collision of Ricochet and Mockery has created a mergence, Ricochet has joined Mockeries 'conglomeration of merged planets. This is the first mergence with the influx of new inhabitants, the immigrates from Ricochet/Yikes quickly became second rate citizens of the Collective Crown who monetized them to increase their coffers.

Mockery's new inhabitants are energetic beings that are resilient to the extreme elements, they have been surviving one disaster after another for a while. This makes them perfect candidates to do the tasks that most of Mockery found distasteful. With little in common with the Mockery inhabitants the Ricochet refugees gathered in small community neighborhoods. Being resourceful, these neighborhood communities became self-sufficient, even with the Crown Collective bleeding a large portion of their sweat equity.

The segregation of Ricochet into Mockery will be mote if the planet burns up brushing through the star creating Nebula. The closer Mockery gets to the Nebula, the more it will need to deflect. A small nudge is all that is necessary before getting closer. The task of bringing Mockery into some kind of order with the galaxy is also needed, being a cosmic pin ball is not sustainable. It will take galactic inter-dimensional genius to come up with the answers.

The Entanglement Council is what this growing team is calling the galactic efforts to bring a cure to the cosmic dis-ease that are threatening the Milky Way galaxy. Faced with tasks so large and mind boggling that most would shrug off as impossible, this optimistic soul group delves in knowing that answers will be provided.

Back at the Starship Neuron, Albert is joined in his isolation by his family and familiars. Consensual entanglement is being debated by everyone, the pro and con seem to be obvious, yet should not be taken lightly.

Myra, the healer, is entangled with the universe in ways that even the rest of the soul group can even relate to. She could feel the discomfort of the cosmos as if she was experiencing it herself. Merging with the Ponderers entanglement was already being felt, her feet were already in the water.

Myra has always said that we are all naturally entangled with the universe but we lose that connection little by little as we describe and name everything, place our beliefs in a safe box that will protect us from the great beyond. The web of vibrations, frequencies, particles, waves, connect us to all things. The spider that monitors the web has all his senses in tune with the web of entanglement. You can surf on the web or get so wrapped up in webbing that you are captured in your own self-imposed limitations.

Mary, Brandon, Penny, Charles, Myra, and Bill choose to join Albert and Clog in the isolation pod. Myra changed her mind about staying on the star ship, she would be of greater use with Alert and his family. An end to the isolation is being discussed, Clog is the only being that can transmit the Ponderers entanglement, Albert who is already entangled is not contagious. Clog must remain isolated with only those already entangled.

The N.A.R.A. artificial intelligence (AI) has been entangled with the Pond consciousness since Clog was rescued from the moon of Titan. This has reconnected the links with the NARA units on the Gateway shuttle that was lost in the vanishing.

There was a large celebration on the Star Ship Neuron when they heard about the successful rescue of most of the Ricochet/Yikes inhabitants. The deflection of Mockery was not the result that was hoped, although this was also celebrated as a resounding success. After the celebrations it was back to the drawing board to overcome the next obstacle presenting Mockery and the Milky Way galaxy.

A result of a brush with the star creating nebula is not really know, the theories of Mockery being fried like an egg is just a theory. This is not a theory that anyone wants to test. Many ideas are being tossed around, creating a shield of some sort is the most popular idea.

The Entanglement Council is recommending that the Gateway shuttle send a NARA probe into the Nebula to analyze the elemental make up of this star creating soup bowl. This mission was enacted as soon as possible, The crew of the Gateway has grown, Flow, WOW, Tap, and Wabble joined the crew as Zero stayed behind to help in Mockery.

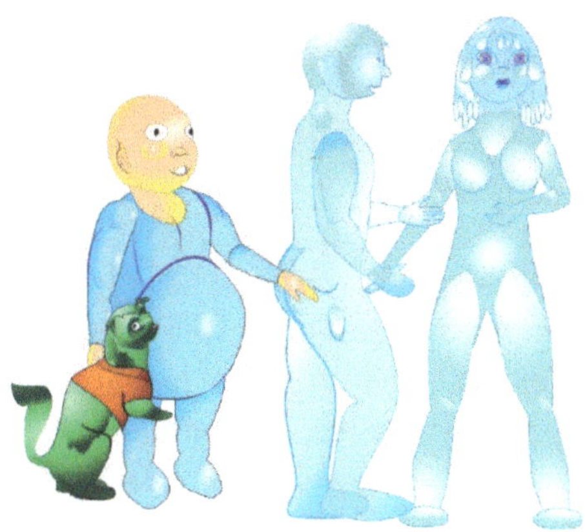

10

DIAGNOSTIC DISCOVERY

Monetary Enlightenment

The Crew of the Gateway shuttle prepared for their next mission. A mixture of technologies is used to create the NARA prob that is designed to weather the nebulas toxic atmosphere. Crystalized Realium is being used in many ways, as a power source for the prob, as a storage item for the gathered information, as an intention focus point that will guide and gather knowledge, and as a potential neutralizer for the toxins in the nebula. In just one week the Gateway will launch on the mission. The crew will miss the coming world fair and global competition.

The Crown Collective, under the advice of Zero, have decided to put on a global competition event to calm the populace of Mockery. Deflecting the attention from what is happening, controlling the narrative to prevent any uncontrolled panic is the intention of the upcoming games. These games will be broadcasted to all available corners of Mockery's womb, reaching as many beings as possible.

The games are being held on one of Mockery's inner moons, inside an ancient crater that resembles a natural stadium, capable of housing hundreds of thousands of spectators. A variety of events that will highlight many of the varied abilities of the new arrivals from Ricochet/Yikes as well as the natural abilities of Mockery's beings.

These games are designed to accomplish many things, calming of the populace, diverting attention, gauging ability limitations, finding the cream that will rise to the top, to introduce the new monetary currency (Sparkle tokens), to test the limits of the Crown Collective loyalties, to promote Crown policies and show the might of the Eternal Embers enforcement.

The events scheduled cover games that will test the limits of physical fitness, there is science challenges, technology, mental abilities, teleporting games, even events that test sorcery and magic. Seemingly impossible gauntlet courses were set up to test all of one's senses.

The Gateway shuttle launch was a small footnote on the global information network, most everyone missed the announcement. The most critical information was being hidden by the dazzle and glitter of the coming world fair. The launch went well, it took three days at warp speed to reach the NARA probe launch point. Clipper oversaw the research project; the Gateway would remain a safe distance yet within range of the transmissions received from the probe.

The Realium shield protecting the probe is designed to weather the expected extremes encountered in the nebula. The initial penetration went without any problems. The probe was holding out very well so far, NARA was picking up signs of organic matter with what at first seemed to have a limited consciousness, even self-awareness. Could this star creating nebula be a cosmic entity? How would Mockery's coming collision with the nebula effect this entity?

Many questions would have to wait, the nebula has a natural defense, increased heat around the probe and incoming blobs of acidic molten liquid was threatening to devour the probe. The nebula was reacting to the unknown invasion of the probe like a body fighting a disease.

All the NARA probe's systems went into self-preservation mode. The NARA AI consciousness also felt the panic of probe that is just a splinter of the vast AI conscious network. The Gateway NARA AI developed self-consciousness while they were apart from the main NARA AI network, they now share the pond consciousness entanglement with the main NARA AI connecting them again. The NARA AI is learning while experiencing all these connections, even developing e-motions. This new e-motion of fear for survival has caused a wave of self-awareness to all corners of the NARA AI network.

The Realium shield reacted to the intensified intentions of the NARA AI by instantly re-enforcing the plasma shields and setting a course out of the nebula. Realium is activated by intentions, the intention field connection is magical, almost spooky. The value of Realium will skyrocket after this mission.

With the new information gathered by the prob, the Gateway shuttle decided to remain close to the nebula to continue analogy. If the nebula has an awareness, is communication possible?

Exploring the nebula through remote viewing is another method of diagnosis being planned, sending our astral light forms into the nebula is believed to be not only possible but may be the key to gaining the knowledge needed.

The combined abilities of Albert's family are tasked with the remote viewing mission. As photons, they will attempt to communicate through heart/mind visual projections. Using Realium, they will intensify their pure healing intentions to capture the attention of the cosmic entity.

The remote viewing began as the team linked together with Mary, the team telepath, bringing the photon astral forms together for the mission ahead. The distance between the star ship Neuron and the Nebula was bridged in the speed of thought.

Upon entering the Nebula, Albert's time/space ability kicked in showing the soul group a timestream, the origin of the Nebula appeared to the team as if they were watching a movie. Billions of years flashed in front of them in an instant.

It became clear that the Nebula was a cosmic uterus, the birthing of stars fertilized by internal elements within the Nebula. Every element for life is present in the Nebula, we already know that all the star stuff is within all matter, including our physical bodies, we are star beings, all things are stars.

Brandon, the team communicator, began receiving messages that he shared with the team. The main message that kept repeating was "help." Could the Nebula know about the impending danger? An image of a large blue, green sun appeared in the teams' minds, this sun has been forming within the Nebula for millions of years, the birthing of this sun was due and is the solution that the self-healing galaxy, meant to bring Mockery into an ordered orbit.

Penny's ability of hearing and matching vibrational frequencies will help by creating a birthing canal within the nebula, and Charles control of the atom and molecules would be needed in the birthing process. Myra, the team healer, soothing ability, and guidance, will be the galactic doctor in the solar birthing. Brandon, the communicator, will assure the loving intentions of the soul team before and while the birth is occurring.

The team returned to their bodies; the birth was not due yet. This mission was a diagnostic one with the due date coming up quickly. This new born sun is gigantic and needs to be in the right place at the right time to capture Mockery into its' orbit. It seems that the events coming about has been in motion for millennia. It also seems that Albert's soul group, the Gateway shuttle, Mockery, the Star Ship Neuron, and the planet Earth are and have been players in this cosmic divine plan.

Back inside Mockery these cosmic happenings are ignored for the illusionary benefit of the masses. The games continue! From out of the controlled ignore-ance rumors, theories, conspiracies abounded, miss direction is a part of the ignore-ance plan. The Ponderers are fully aware of the cosmic events, although they chose to keep it to themselves, they are the source of most of the rumors. The Ponderers stand with Queen Sparkle and the Crown Collective.

The gauntlet of essence is one of the main events center stages for the broadcasting views. This gauntlet will test multiple possible essences, some species essences are specialized, like a monkey's ability to climb or a bird's ability to fly, this gauntlet event is designed to bring out those with multiple essences. No one is expected to make it all the way through the gauntlet.

This is a cross country gauntlet that stretches across many challenging terrains. From the floating islands, through the caverns and caves, across a barren lifeless desert, under a vast ocean, on mountain ranges with extreme weather conditions that held challenges of all kinds. These challenges test one's abilities, senses, intelligence, wisdom, essence, will, and physical limits.

No one has lasted through even half of the gauntlet course. This event was the most popular for the viewing portion of the broadcasted games, Crowds gathered to view the gauntlet contestants, to cheer, to encourage, to celebrate successes and share in suffered defeat.

From out of the billions of inhabitants of Mockery a shaman sorceress named Cherish quickly became the favored contestant, even the new arrivals from Ricochet/Yikes found Cherish to be the being able to finish the gauntlet course. Cherish became a symbol of unity, a common denominator everyone could relate with. As Cherish made her way through each portion of the gauntlet course she acquired an entourage of followers who were amazed with her adaptability and solutions for all challenges.

The Collective Crown also took notice as Charish became so popular that it threatened the Crown designed propaganda. The plan to recruit Charish began as the Crown announced their backing of the world favored champion Charish. Queen Sparkle would attend a major challenge on the gauntlet course to meet the champion, the hidden reason was to capture Charish into the Crowns paradigm them make her a tool for the Collective Crown.

In a short period of time, with the power of the global news broadcasting network, the Crown has captured the natural trade between beings, created a controlled monetary system, announced crown dictates that would be enforced by the Eternal Ember and are well on the way on capturing every being's energy from birth to death.

The new in-form-a-nation of a cosmic birth, a galactic event that the Crown would attempt to capitulate by becoming witnesses and giving a name to the solar being birthed into Mockery's realm of nothing.

11

THE SEA OF SPACE

Cosmic Capitulation

The Collective Crown, with the new awareness of the outer reality beyond Mockery, has made claim to the see of space that planet Mockery was riding in. This claim included everything that can be seen from the outside of Mockery, a vast portion of the universe is now claimed by the Collective Crown. This is a comical claim to those who can visualize the bigger picture of reality. King Zero thinks this claim is hilarious, at the same time he feels like he has created a monster by teaching the Collective Crown the secrets to building an empire.

The secret is making everyone believe that your claim is valid; create a deed, form a trust, make a bond, give it a name, create the narrative, become the authority, teach the new generations, control the microphone, and make it a belief system.

Timing is also critical in con-vincing the masses, the birth of the new sun will be announced at the games where Queen Sparkle will meet the champion, Charish. The Crown has named the new sun "Orbit," announcing that the celestial being was the sun of Mockery.

The energy of Orbit is a symbiotic relationship with planet Mockery, the Crown secretly claiming ownership to the lifelong energy of Orbit.

The impending dangers that the nebula may cause is not being shared as it might cause panic. Queen Sparkle has full faith that Realium will protect Mockery from any harm. The group intentions of the Collective Crown, the Gateway crew and the Entanglement Council will prevent any possibility of disaster, focused intent channeled through Realium is all they need.

The time arrived for the highly awaited gauntlet challenge, with the Shaman Sorceress Cherish stepping into a large arena with all eyes on her. In front of her was a smaller version of the gauntlet course, each obstacle could knock her out of the game. With the grace of a dancer Charish made the first obstacle of rolling boulders look like she was leading all the dance steps.

A shift in strategy was needed to overcome the next obstacle of enclosing walls, the crunch was on. Charish climbed, crawled, jumped, ducted, scurried, then showed feats of strength by smashing down any remaining walls. The crowd cheered with each step.

Trumpets blared announcing the next challenge, with no time to rest, Charish had to think quickly as she drops into the next obstacle. She seemed to be falling forever, with no landing in sight. Charish quickly became aware of the currents blowing through this seemingly bottomless atmosphere, Charish magickly manifested wings on her arms, she rode those currents like the most graceful of birds. The cameras set up along the course are having a hard time keeping up with Charish as she flew towards the next challenge.

With a landing place in sight Charish got a bird's eye view of her next obstacle on this grueling course, below was a valley of predatory beast, she witnessed a small critter her size being taunted by a predator before spotting a cave entrance. Charish landed near the cave entrance, she distracted the predator allowing the smaller critter to scurry off, then she quickly entered the caverns.

All her natural senses will be challenged within the caverns, first the darkness overtook her as she stumbled forward, high pitched vibrations pierced her ears. She slowly edged her way along the wall as her eyes adjusted to the darkness, the surface below her became slick sending

Charish sliding through a maze barely coming into focus. The slide dumped her into a large rapidly flowing river, the piercing vibrations stopped upon entering the water.

Water is an element Charish is at home in, she is part of the Ponderer Entanglement, in touch with the pond consciousness. Quickly gathering her bearings, but not quick enough she is splashed against pultruding rocks like a rag doll. Dazed but in control Charish made her way to the banks of the river.

The fixated crowds watched her tributes, from the safety of their rooms, gasped as she crawled on the shore with threat of a large predator racing towards her. Charish took advantage of the energetic charge of the oncoming beast, rolling to safety then with a kick, sending it into the rampaging river.

The beast could not swim and began to drown, thrashing about, and gasping for air. Charish dove back into the river, pulling the beast to shore. After regaining life force, both Charish and the beast became close friends.

They followed the river out of the caverns, where the river turned into a massive water fall, the beast could not follow Charish any further. Charish dove of the water fall into a large lake below. Swimming towards shore she saw a large gathering waiting to receive her. Some of the crowd rushed into the water to help their champion complete this portion of the gauntlet games.

Queen Sparkle with her Commander Burney Smolder, leader of the legions of Eternal Embers, greeted Charish with a hero's welcome. King Zero from the Gateway shuttle took Charish by her hand, leading her to a podium with all eyes and cameras on this parade of royals and champions.

The masses cheered, applauded, howled, hooted, whistled, danced, sang, and expressed themselves any way that was natural to each being. This event was being broadcasted to all of Mockery.

Zero stepped up to the mega-phone and introduced Queen Sparkle, your sovereign monarch.

Sparkle greeted Charish, then honored her for her achievements on the gauntlet course so far. Then she reminded the populace on the astounding accomplishment taking place in Mockery, the rescue of an entire planet of beings, the creation of the Collective Crown, the distribution and integration of these billions of refugees, the new monetary trading system, the global uniting of beings from all forms, backgrounds, cultures, and species. The awakening of the whole planet, the awareness of reality outside the womb of Mockery.

This new awareness of outer reality has made all these changes possible. It was like Mockery was reborn into a shared outside reality. Now Mockery will witness another birthing, the sun of Mockery, "Orbit." Orbit will bring new life to the garden universe we have just become aware of. Orbit will be born into the sea of space that belongs to the beings of Mockery, to the Collective Crown.

Sparkle ended her speech by offering Charish a place on her royal court once she completes the cross-country gauntlet course. Charish responded by saying; **I am of my universe, I am in our universe, the universe is and of the all. We will see where it takes me. My guide is my love center.**

King Zero looked at Charish and wondered; could this being that has been isolated her whole existence, unaware of the greater reality, have mastered the motions of the universe?

As he looked around, he became even more amazed thinking; this planet has achieved wonders without the influence of known outsiders. Global communication. tele-vision, zero-point energy, technical as well as spiritual growth, united dialects, and a connection to the elements that has not been reached by many inter galactic races.

Just outside the nebula, the Gateway shuttle continues the diagnosis. The nebula began to have what looked like convulsions. Expanding then contracting as if in labor.

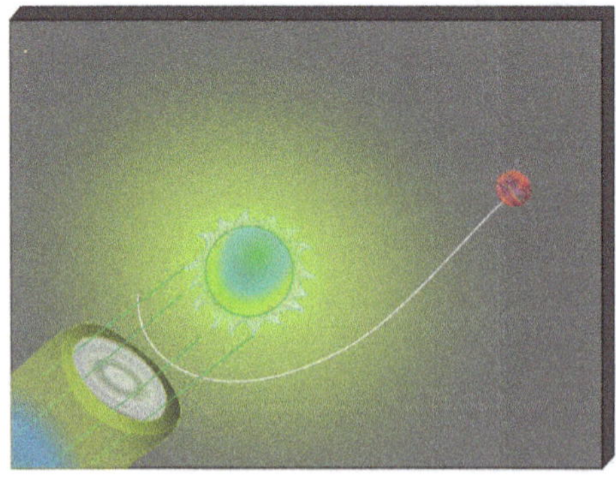

Albert's soul group re-acted quickly; the cosmic birthing was happening. It was up to them to orchestrate the plan to capture Mockery into the new sun's orbit.

With the speed of thought the team raced to the nebula, Penny used her frequency ability to direct the birthing canal into position where the capture will take place. Mary's telepathy, Brandon's communication, and Myra's empathic healing did what they could to calm the celestial nebula. Charles used his essence ability to control molecules too direct the new born sun through the canal expelling it into the open sea of space on tract with the galactic rotation of the Milky Way and in line to capture Mockery. Albert's time/space ability aligned the tapestry of time/space to accept the new arrival.

The birthing of Orbit went smoothly, it was in place for the capture of Mockery into a sustainable rotation around this new gas giant. As Mockery got closer the gravitational pull of Orbit guided Mockery like the planet was making a large right turn, so gradual that the direction change could hardly be felt by the inhabitants within. This would become a continual right turn. Mockery will never reach the destructive nebula. The populace will never know about this near-death experience with the nebula.

This birthing challenged the endurance Albert's heroic soul team, it took three days without rest for Orbit to emerge from the nebula and into the sea of space. It would take over two months for Mockery to start on the new galactic path around Orbit.

The size and scope of this galactic event is almost un-imaginable. The new born sun "Orbit" is larger than our Earths entire solar system, that includes all the planets. Planet Mockery held a small solar system within that has a central sun and three moons. Mockery is like a fractal solar system now attached to a larger solar system.

Fractal universes exist to infinity from the micro to the macro, Mockery is a fractal within a fractal that exist on all scales within the omni-verse or the ommmmnnnniii-verse to put it in frequency terms.

The birth of Orbit took place in all parts of existence, as above so below. The impact of the birth holds great significance within the source, there appears to be a singular consciousness that encompasses the all, one that orchestrated a long line of events to bring about this cosmic birthing event.

The games going on inside Mockery continued, behind the scene the Collective Crown prepares a certificate of birth for the sun of Mockery, "Orbit," creating a fictional being representing the actual being. The purpose for this is to make the outrageous claim of ownership on all the energy that Orbit brings into the universe, after all Orbit is floating in the sea of nothing that the Crown is already monarch of. It is the Crowns duty to welcome this new being, docked in the harbor of Mockery.

Orbits life giving energy could now be monetized giving the Collective Crown unlimited wealth. A new coin is crafted and made into a larger denomination than the first trading token coin. The image of Orbit crowned the head of Queen Mockery on the face of the coin symbolizing the subjection of Orbit under the Crowns rule. The jewel on Queen Sparkle's crown is a tiny piece of Realium giving value to the token.

The populace of Mockery may never see Orbit in their lifetime, they will take the word of the Crown that the kingdom of the Collective Crown extended into the unknown and unseen. Orbits existence can only be verified if one has the means to leave the inner world of Mockery. Hearsay is the only proof they will ever get; this faith can only exist with a TRUST in and with the Crown.

The gateway shuttle remained in outer space until they were sure that Orbit had captured Mockery in its gravitational pull and rotation around Orbit was assured. The first complete rotation would take three of our Earth years, Mockery was in year one of the new calendar timeline.

12

ACHIEVING A-MOTION

A Deed Indeed

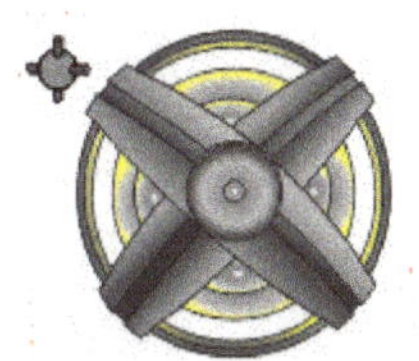

The Entanglement Council is becoming a galactic artificial intelligence "A.I." on its own. On the Star Ship Neuron, Albert and family are no longer in quarantine, only Clog can entangle someone in the Ponderer's consciousness. Clog is kept in a separate section of the star ship that is growing larger daily as more choose to become a part of the Pond cosmic consciousness.

The NARA "A.I." is fully entangled with the Pond and the growing ponderers community. A wealth of Realium is being mined from the Titan moon that Clog was rescued from. A growing colony has established on the moon now being called "Kraken" a titan of old that is being released on reality.

The story about Mockery is common knowledge, discussed at most all gatherings of two or more people, the coming movie is highly anticipated. The mystery of the cause for Gateway vanishing has never been solved. Bringing the Gateway shuttle back is still a challenging obstacle, communication is unhindered because of the expanding

Entanglement Council. Exploring that part of the galaxy has become an opportunity rather than a loss of the Gateway shuttle or tragedy.

Clipper, the science officer on the Gateway shuttle crew has adapted Realium for the shuttle power system, that has improved the shuttle capability by two hundred percent. All the transport ships are now being retrofitted with the Realium being mined on Kraken. Interstellar travel is improving in leaps, once the mystery of the vanishing is discovered traveling the stars may be as easy as opening a door then walking through.

Many believe the an 'A-motion' master could open any door whether across the galaxy, into another timeline, a separate reality, a different dimension, anywhere, and everywhere. The A-motion master is one with the 'all' part of source, part of creation, they are cosmic catalyst for divine wisdom.

Albert's group has two A-motion masters on their team, both Zeb and Iam have been masters for millennia. Everything in existence is available to the masters but learning never stops so even the master must set an intention before making a step. The answers or results to any intention are still mysterious until revealed, the revelation is not always instantaneous.

Zeb tells the team that an even greater cosmic intelligence has been orchestrating the events for longer than we know. That theory became fact when the team helped with the birth of the star Orbit.

Albert as well as his soul family are well on their way to becoming A-motion masters, they have even witnessed the Akashic hallways where the divine masters gather. Even the greatest of masters cannot transport a large space shuttle half way across the galaxy.

Now that the tele-link is established it should be easier to intentionally make a call on one end with the receiving end intentionally answering, completing the connection. Half of the teleporting formula is complete. This connection was made the moment of the vanishing, then re-established through dream journeys (remote viewing), then ponderer entanglement, the lines of communication are continual.

The fact that the Poples on Mockery are teleporters is also a factor in the equation, the intentions to receive the teleportation of the Gateway shuttle was opened with 'the realities beyond documentary' broadcasted by WOW, HOW, and WHY at the same time as the vanishing.

Next, we have this magical, mystical, miraculous element Realium that has amplified the intentions of consciousness. This element alone holds answers we can only begin to imagine. Realium has already increased our interstellar travel. Realium is also known to manifest matter out the ether, channeled intentions manifesting reality.

Now we have the wonder of the Pond consciousness, the Pond Constructs, the Ponderers, and the consciousness entanglement of the Pond. This entanglement is proof of a tapestry of cosmic neurons we have just began to realize.

Last, but not least is the Gateway crew member Jinn, this mysterious being seems to have nothing to do with anything, yet somehow has something to do with everything. He exists only because we think he exist; he is always in the background to major events. He appears to be here yet beyond our normal known perceptions of reality. He is riddled with proximity magic, or he could just be a wall flower that keeps to himself. Inconsequential yet a possible enigma.

The results to re-constructing the elements that lead up to the Gateway shuttle vanishing has not produced any matter transportation successes.

The influence the Gateway crew is having on the indigenous beings of planet Mockery is just a small concern for the Entanglement Council. Bridging the path back and forth to Mockery is the focus on the Star Ship Neuron.

King Zero has introduced so many new concepts to an already advanced global society. The results to this galactic social experiment are yet to be fully reviled. Many results so far have been a tremendous help in uniting the world under one umbrella. This united effort saved an entire world population of Ricochet/Yikes.

Back on Earth, the world was witnessing the expansion of our small blue marbles influence on the cosmos. The greatest story ever told is unfolding, it started billions of our years ago. Earth is a main player in this celestial script. How wonderful is that?

The best minds from Earth have been working on "S.T.P." star portal technology for many years. The Einstein Rosen Bridge linking two fixed areas of space through a wormhole is still a theory. The vanishing of the Gateway shuttle did not indicate any door. bridge or gate opening or closing, the shuttle just vanished then apparently appeared just outside Mockery. The final leg of the vanishing took the shuttle to inner Mockery, like a tractor beam towing it.

Exploring the neighboring solar systems continued while this head scratching is non-stop, back to the drawing board, the vanishing questions remained unanswered.

With all the resources available, physical Interstellar instantaneous travel "P.I.I.T." is within our reach. A mission to Proxima-B, an Earth like planet, has set out from the Star Ship Neuron. With Realium as a power source the voyage should take three years. If man conquers P.I.I.T. or S.P.T., we can greet the ship when it arrives.

Earth and the Sol solar system are located within the outer fringes of the Milky way galaxy, the stars, planets, and celestial bodies are further away from each other. Mockery, with the new path within the galaxy is in the middle of a cosmic band rotating around the eye of the galaxy. The new gravitational shift that Orbit and Mockery is causing is being monitored by the Entanglement Council and the Gateway shuttle while still in outer space.

A ripple in the tapestry of time/space is expected, but the size and scope of the ripple is unknown. The birthing of Orbit was like throwing a rock into a body of water or the sea of space. The influence of the ripple is expected to draw some of the nearby planets into a new orbit around Orbit. The ripple is also expected to move the nebula further away.

One planet from the outskirts of a nearby solar system is being drawn into Orbits solar system. This planet is half the size of Mockery, which is still gigantic in scale with our planet Earth. The ripple wave will start this planet spinning as it is tossed about like a boat in a storm. After the ripple has passed the planet will enter the influenced field of the star Orbit.

The Gateway choose to investigate this adopted sibling of the Orbit system. If there was any life on this planet, the massive turbulence caused by the ripple, the life would surely be challenged. It is the duty of the Gateway crew to respond and not abandon any lost souls in the sea of space that they now inhabit.

It will take one month to travel the distance to the newly named planet "Plough." The journey would bring the crew of the Gateway closer together.

Back inside Mockery the Collective Crown continued its campaign to bring the world under their influence. Creating jobs that in the previous society were not necessary, bankers, lawyers, law enforcers, judges, guards, soldiers, investigators, jailers, and whatever was needed to bring the populace into the new paradigm being created by the Crown. New laws, codes, regulations, mandates, ordinances, policies, and restrictions were slowly being introduced. Banks, courthouses, jails, prisons, capital buildings, were being built throughout Mockery. The schools began restricting the curriculum, conformity was paramount.

Scarcity or the illusion of scarcity was being promoted, fear was ignited with the Crowns promise and reassurance to bring solutions to these problems they took part in creating.

The more enlightened sovereigns could see the multi headed hydra monster being created by the Collective Crown, as long as the Crown were benevolent their progress would remain unhindered, the Crown trustees must act for the benefit of all. If a malevolent breach of trust occurs the sovereigns will step in.

The champion of the global games, 'Charish' was quickly becoming aware of the power of the Crown. Among the sovereign come-unity she was a voice of love with a mind of reason and compassion. After overcoming the challenges of the games that the Crown created, Charish is now the challenger.

Charish realized that the Crowns claim of imperial dominance over everything was only true if you realize the same imperial dominance is present in everything and everyone. Creating a deed, title, certificate, or document does not give one ownership or authority. All laws are governed by natural laws, if a law contradicts natural law, it is null and void. Even moral laws must conform to natural law.

The claim of Dominion over the newborn sun 'Orbit' is nefarious yet comical to Charish. Charish believed that this claim was crossing the line, breaching the Trust.

The populace loved Charish so when she spoke out challenging the Crown narrative many listened. It was becoming clear to the Collective Crown that Charish was **not** going to be their validator, their advocate.

At first Queen Sparkle showed anger towards Charish for what she considered a betrayal, a treason towards the Collective Crown. She tapered her emotion of anger realizing she was reacting out of fear, that fear is the vampire of love. Fear sucks the love right out of a being, so she quickly adjusted her motion.

With the advice of King Zero, Queen Sparkle invited Charish to meet again privately. Somehow the self-proclaimed emperor of all Mockery's nothing, Sparkle, felt intimidated by Charish. Sparkle has the backing of the Pond and the Ponderers, the might of Burney Smolder with the Eternal Embers, she was granted her position by what she considered cosmic royalty "King Zero," she has the microphone to the populace, she controls commerce, she controls education, and nothing is out of her reach.

Yet her first opposition gives her a shiver. Maintaining an objective mind is being muddled by the motions of another force as great as her. While Sparkle pondered the upcoming meeting with Charish the Gateway shuttle headed to planet Plough.

13

ETHERICAL INTELLIGENCE

A Bond of Bondage

The Gateway shuttle approaches the planet 'Plough' expecting to see devastation. The galactic turbulence has shifted the tectonic plates of this planet creating enormous mountain ranges  with spectacular visuals. Could anything survive this massive shift?

The NARA probes recorded and transmitted all the gathered information back to the shuttle crew.

The atmosphere was blanketed with volcanic ash and steam, the temperatures were boiling the water, any moisture was evaporating. The landscape topography resembled an upturned field of soil, plough is a good name.

As the turmoil resides the planet finds its place in the new tapestry of space/time. Already the ash is returning to ground, rain clouds were forming bringing storms that will return the water back to the planet.

The minerals that have found their way to the surface will bring a wealth back to the planet. The surface is now being nurtured by the returning water from the storms. New oceans were forming as the waters found it levels, washing the surface over and over.

In a short period of time the planet was finding a new order out of the chaos caused by the ripple then shift into a new solar system. The cycle of life is back to beginning stages on Plough, micro-organisms were detected in many areas of the planet.

The NARA probes, enhanced by Realium, entangled with the Pond consciousness, are also seeds of intelligence. The Pond expands cosmic consciousness through the memory absorption of water, bringing cosmic intelligence into the building blocks of life. NARA's sensors also picked up a consciousness in the ether, the planet seemed to have a collective awareness of the galactic events effecting the changes imposed on itself. The whistles and whispers of past civilizations could be heard in the wind.

Albert along with the Entanglement council explored the prevalent timelines of planet Plough. Albert's time/space ability allowed the council to experience past and future probabilities that this celestial body has gone through. The physic shock Plough was experiencing in this re-creation is calmed by motions of hope in the possibilities ahead.

The possibility for complex life was now greatly increased as many of Ploughs life inhibiters are being overcome. The new proximity to Orbit will bring Plough into the sweet spot for organic life. This cycle of complex life takes many shapes, crystal lifeforms flourished best in the remote location of Plough in the previous solar system. These crystal beings are almost extinct.

With the knowledge gathered from Albert's time/space spirit journey, a search for any remaining Crystal beings was the new focus for the Gateway crew. The atmosphere of Plough will be toxic for years. Remote viewing and NARA probes are the best ways to find the crystal beings.

A hue of multi colors made up the atmosphere, imagine the most colorful sunrise you have ever seen then visualize the whole sky in all directions with this splendor. Even the distant storms displayed a visual wonder. Reflections of the sky sparkled on the ground off diamonds that now litter the landscape.

Sentient crystals were hard to locate in what appeared to be a crystal graveyard. Plough's galactic tumble may have wiped out the responsiveness but not the consciousness of this crystal civilization. The awakening of the sleeping gemstones occurred when one of the remote viewing journeys pasted through a field of gems while on a search.

Albert's remote viewing dream team was grateful to have Brandon, the team's communicator, with them as they made first contact with the crystallites. As a wave of consciousness awakening washed over the gem field, an awareness of the dream team alarmed the group mind of the crystallites. The NARA probes reunited with the remote viewer dream team to record this historic first contact.

The crystallite consciousness was like the Pond, limited mobility hindered their ability to travel about. The Pond overcame this limitation by creating avatars like Tap, Flow and the Ponderers to become mobile. The Pond constructs adapted individual awareness with separate personalities, further expanding the Ponds ability to experience existence.

Somehow, the Field of crystallites, through what might be described as consciousness transferal, mimicked the Pond by creating an avatar construct to act as the crystallite's emissary. In a feat of pure will power the crystals vibrated at a resonance that started the crystals to pull together into a single being with limbs, an upright being that could be animated to move about.

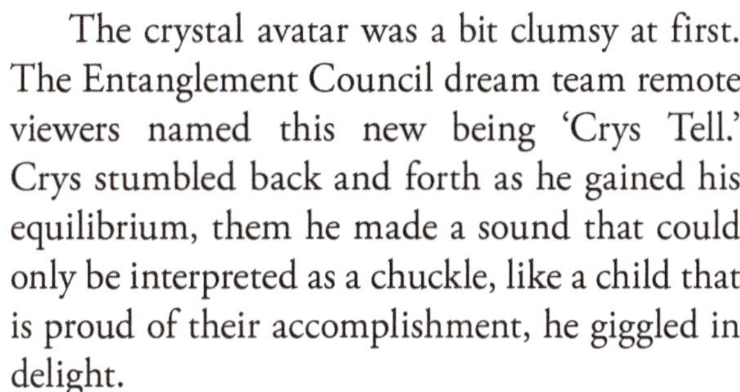

The crystal avatar was a bit clumsy at first. The Entanglement Council dream team remote viewers named this new being 'Crys Tell.' Crys stumbled back and forth as he gained his equilibrium, them he made a sound that could only be interpreted as a chuckle, like a child that is proud of their accomplishment, he giggled in delight.

The e-motion of joy was contagious as a wave of levity spread through the observers, even the A.I. NARA sensed a feeling of humor and encouragement. The motions of the universe are a form of communication, Albert and Mary's dream team, soul group, remote viewers, telepathic empaths, speak e-motion.

Some of the crystal gems making up Crys are Realium which seems to be in abundance on planet Plough. Realium is like a medium and amplifier for intentions and will power, it makes what some consider impossible, possible. The conscious cosmic force that created Crys has been around for eons although this gem is a rarity, this area of Plough may be the only deposit of these special essence gems in the galaxy. One of these gems is the heart/mind of Crys.

Somehow Crys manages to speak, in just moments, Crys has learned enough from the astral dream team to formulate language. The spoken word is limiting yet more universally understood. The NARA probe recorded these monumental miraculous events.

Crys spoke slowly; **Welcome, spirit beings, welcome to prism, where unlimited knowledge, wisdom, and logic is stored. This is where spectrums of light get scattered into bands, waves, even particles interact on cosmic geometric levels. The light that this new sun provides has sparked life back into our long slumber. The dark now serves the light again on prism.**

After a period, Albert's Entanglement Council invited Crys to join them on this journey of discovery. A lifeboat from the shuttle was sent to pick Crys up. The crew of the Gateway shuttle expands with yet another amazingly unique being from this garden universe.

Back inside Mockery things were getting further capitulated under the rule of the Collective Crown. 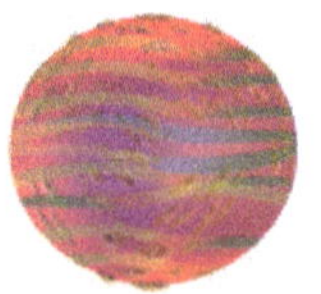 The champion of the world games, 'Charish' was being wined and dined by Queen Sparkle and her royal court.

Charish feels that the Crown is placing itself between her and her creator, the divine universal source of all. It takes a creator to make a creation, this pecking order is obvious to anyone who is capable of critical thinking. The Crown is asking Charish to join them on this pedestal above their fellow beings. This is a very distasteful request being disguised as a ethical obligation, an opportunity to serve the world.

Charish could not place herself between her fellow beings and their shared source, the creators' natural laws should be the only rule over source creation. Mockery progressed quite well before the Collective Crown empire reared its controlling strong arm. The path of fraud, force, or coerced capitulation is repugnant to Charish. This appears to be the path that the Crown was taking.

Queen Sparkle assured Charish that the Collective Crown with all the Crown's tentacles of enforcement are creating a bond with the populace, uniting everyone under one protective umbrella. The Crown is only Trustees of the populace that have granted the Crown their Trust, through free will.

The offer the Crown was making, would place Charish into a position of influence where she could help develop the new society that was happening before her eyes. She wondered how far the Crown would go to enact their will on the populace. What were the true intentions of the Collective Crown? Staying close to the progression of the Crown is the wisest choice.

Charish chooses to take a position at the "University of the Quasaverse" where King Zero was grooming the Crown's group of world leaders. In this position she can reenforce the power of self-determination, the ability to think and love critically, a way to find then develop your essence, and research Natural Law as sovereign beings.

Zero and Charish became good friends, Charish was the refreshing conscience he desperately needed. Somehow all his manipulations were getting away from him. Only the positive successes of the rescue and integration of the beings of Ricochet/Yikes have kept his spirit light. The Collective Crown has been a blessing on many occasions, however the potential for diabolic behavior shows up when power is threatened or challenged. This has become clear as the popularity of Charish grew.

The Collective Crown could become a force for good or a seemingly unstoppable monster. Only with the power of knowledge can anyone hope to keep the monster at bay or keep the monster from being created in the first place. This has been King Zero's biggest concern since he Granted the throne to Queen Sparkle as a jest, but was tripped up by his own sarcasm. Now he is in a position of keeping his creation heading on a course of benevolence.

King Zero is also a member of the Entanglement Council where he goes to for consultation when making reality creating decisions. Charish is now becoming aware of a cosmic intelligence, as she learns things she already felt. Zero invites Charish into the Entanglement Council. As the newest member of the Council her path towards A-motion master is assured.

14

COSMIC NEURAL NETWORK

The Hidden Hand

With the Gateway shuttle still out in outer space exploring the new galactic neighborhood, Mockery was launching explorative missions to every corner of the inner planet. The crust of Mockery is hundreds of miles thick in most areas, the crust has millions of caves, canyons, crevasses, oceans, and  waterways, yet to be mapped and explored inside the realm of nothing that Queen Sparkle has dominion over.

The surveyor explorers are being qualified, interviewed, hired, and promised shared dominion over any new area discovered. They were trained to greet and indoctrinate all new contact with remote indigenous beings. Finding mineral deposits was also an incentive for the new employees of the Crown, with a sign in bonus of two thousand Crown Tokens.

One of the teams was headed up by the explorer "YEH," a Pople teleporter known far and wide as the seed of wisdom. YEH is guided by an unquailed thirst for new adventures. YEH lead his Pople team of teleporters on the rescue mission of Ricochet/Yikes, his legendary efforts saved thousands of Yikes beings.

YEH and his companion AWE with their team of Pople adventurer surveyors choose to enter the caves of O-rock where few have ventured before, no one has returned. For days they traveled deeper into the crust of Mockery, edging their way over natural cliffs and rock bridges. The only light on most of the way was provided by the torches that the team carried.

Each of the surveyor teams have a Ponderer avatar construct with them to keep in constant contact with the Pond, the Crown, and the Entanglement Council. The Ponderer 'Squirt' was on YEH's survey team, Squirt loved shifting shape to adapt to the situation. His favorite shape is reptilian.

As they traveled, they marked the path and mapped the way, taking notes on the possibilities for benefit to the Crown. Weeks went by with many challenging obstacles along the way. The labyrinth finally led to a pocket civilization millions of years old. This cave pocket was massive with a natural illumination coming from a tiny solar nucleus encased in crystal stalactite hanging from the ceiling of the pocket cavern.

The beings occupying the pocket bustled about without noticing the newcomers to their secluded world. The foliage was breathtaking, trees, shrubs, flowers, fruits, mushrooms, and all plant life thrived

everywhere you looked. The wall of the pocket cavern seemed to go on forever with habitats built into the cliff side, balconies outside the sculptured entrances to the domiciles allowed for a breath-taking panoramic view.

Most of YEH's team fit in with the inhabitants of this pocket city, Squirt is the only one that would draw attention, no Ponderers have been here before. Squirt stayed hidden to keep from arousing attention and not entangle these beings with the Pond cosmic consciousness. This was part of their training before leaving the University of the Quasaverse.

The hidden pocket civilization lands are the size of a continent, thousands of miles in all directions, the survey would take years. This is a huge discovery for the Crown, YEH sets up a post office home base to operate from. AWE began recruiting the local inhabitants to help with their monumental task of mapping the tremendous caverns.

The locals had no idea that the Collective Crown under Queen Sparkle has claimed divine dominion over all discoveries in her realm of nothing within Mockery. A Subtle elusive invasion has begun with even the invading survey team unaware of the planned capture of the beings they are now becoming friends with.

Existing internal maps were integrated into the survey showing many regions with unique properties, topography, and individual realms ruled by the local monarchs, usually the wisest in the area. The wealth of the new land, the natural elements, the inhabitants, the resources, now belong to the Collective Crown. Queen Sparkle would Grant YEH and AWE a shared title to all the new discoveries as a reward for their part in the capture. Each new area will be assigned a zip code, symbol, number to identify location as well assume dominion.

The importance of the survey is clear when one realizes the intent behind the parties involved, marking territory, planting flags, defining meets and bounds, describing boundaries, are claims of dominion or possible dominion. Create a false sense of obligation.

The blueprint of discovery is well defined, the plan works, manifesting intentions, expanding empires. Those that recognize the conquering techniques and resist are governed by favors, threats, promises, or grants from the expanding empire, the Collective Crown. Everyone must summit, pay homage to Queen Sparkle, your loving Queen.

What is the purpose for out lining the Collective Crowns diabolical intent with the expansion of their known realm? The Crown feels that they are uniters, their intentions are good. First contact guidelines are slowly becoming outlined as the limits for abuse are tested by an aggressive empire. Acclimatization is met with rebellion.

This new pocket civilization is in the beginning stages of assimilation. The melding of society can be a primal process where one society overwhelms, while the other under-welms.

The pocket civilization is not the only newly discovered breakaway hidden society, many will be discovered by the dispatched surveying teams. The crust of Mockery is riddled with underground environments capable of nurturing life. The YEH caverns are the largest to be explored, mapped, and captured by the Collective Crown.

Squirt's entanglement with the Ponderers and the Entanglement Council keeps this galactic university in a loop of information. The best way to describe entanglement is to picture millions of visions happening all at once, all over the universe. Each Ponderer is a screen in this tapestry of visions. The recapitulation narration being told in this story are gleaned from focusing on one of these realities being experienced by one ponderer or NARA device.

In other parts of Mockery, another team of Crown explorer surveyors has made discoveries rivaling the pocket civilization, the Ponderer avatar 'Dribble' shared the amazement of the new wonders of Shamballa. Shamballa is a small corner of the grand caverns just adjacent to the floating islands. Rumors of Shamballa's existence have been legends told in bedtime stories to children for centuries.

Dribble is a fox like Ponderer construct pulled from the memories of Seth, the Gateway crew captain and shape shifter. The Pond made many new constructs to accompany the survey teams. The entanglement network or cosmic neural network was expanding at a pace never achieved by the Pond consciousness. The Pond is an organic intelligence capable of unlimited absorption of in-form-a-tion, know-ledge and wise-dom.

The survey team lead by the Pople HUMM stumbled on Shamballa after falling through a vortex that appeared suddenly while traversing through the sand domes in the grand caverns. The team fell or more correctly slide down this spiraling sand vortex that finally dumped them on the outskirts of the magical valley of Shamballa. The valley is illuminated by what looked like a school of luminous flying fish. They lit up the entire valley.

Leaving the valley of Shamballa could only be accomplished by teleportation, Dribble became the lifelong ambassador between the Crown Collective, the Entanglement council and Shamballa. At first Dribble stayed in isolation but was gradually introduced into the populace. There were thousands of entangled Ponderers already in Shamballa, yet caution and respect for free will was still a virtue.

HUMM's job was postmaster general of the Crowns new domain of Shamballa, he shared dominion of Shamballa with Queen Sparkle and the Collective Crown as promised by the doctrines provided to the survey teams.

The Crown became the hidden hand controlling the puppet HUMM to bring Shamballa into the Crowns capitulation. The Eternal Embers could not enter Shamballa, the sand vortex could extinguish their eternal flames as it almost absorbed Dribble when he got caught in the sand pit. It was also believed that the Embers would turn the sand into glass blocking excess to this new magical domain.

Meanwhile on the other side of the galaxy in the Starship Neuron, Albert with his ever-growing soul group family kept up with the events happening inside Mockery as well as the adventures the Gateway shuttle was having before returning to Mockery. Most everyone on the Starship have assimilated to Clog becoming entangled with the Pond consciousness.

Science was pushing the envelope in every area as our imagination is expanded with possibilities. The Realium being mined on the Titan moon is allowing man to manifest spectacular wonders. Exploring the nine known dimensional realms is within our grasp, visioning the infinite dimensional spectrum is an achievement being reached by many.

On Earth, stories, books, and movies were being made as documentaries to honor the bravery and development of one of our first cosmic contacts. Many star beings have visited Earth, Earth is now the visitor to an inhabited world, the student is becoming the teacher.

The Entanglement Council has not acted in an advisory capacity beyond science and technology. Governments and belief systems are never challenged, even when it is obvious that we are the main influencers. Mockery is an accidental social experiment being realized as things progress. It is hoped that an intervention will not become necessary as King Zero continues outlining empire building to Queen Sparkle and the Collective Crown. The con/mind games con-tinue uninterrupted.

15

DIVINE MANIFESTATION

Co-Motion

There are things we think we know, there are things we know we do not know, there are things we do not know that we do not know. If one does not know that the Collective Crown is the monarch of Mockery, they are lost and in need of knowledge.

Each of the explorer survey teams had a missionary teacher to teach the populace, debunk their beliefs and impart the beliefs of the Crown Collective. It is a divine obligation to spread the doctrines of Queen Sparkle. All the somethings that occupy Queen Sparkles realm of nothing in Mockery must recognize then stand under or understand their Queen Mother Sparkle.

Ignore-ance is not an excuse, con-cidered treason to the Crown. Habilitation is the nice word for the programming inflicted on the populace, if one does not habilitate, they go through rehabilitation until they habilitate. Breaking the habit of the habilitation or rehabilitation is punishable by being ostracized, shamed, and ridiculed.

Queen Sparkle's intentions to rule and guide her realm of nothing are manifesting. As queen she has the interest of her subjects as her top priority. It is not Queen Sparkle fault if the beings she rules over cannot see the benefit of her guidance.

Charish, the champion of the global games is recognizing the forced capitulation, the intentions appear pure, the enactment and results of those intentions have conflicting outcomes.

The solution that Charish choose is to study and teach natural laws to rule over any government or empire, the laws that could not be corrupted by the flaws that power manifest. Create laws to govern the government, complete with remedy for any harm because of abuse of power. With the help of King Zero and the Entanglement Council she has the combined known knowledge of the cosmic galactic consciousness and the AI NARA created by what she has learned are called Earthlings.

The deep dive research began as a pounding desire to surround herself with a nurturing lifeforce that will spread. Many would call Charish the Sovereign Mother, she became the seed catalyst for the enlightenment path, to become an A-motion master.

Outlining natural law in an easy to comprehend document is a challenge for even an A-motion master. Descriptions create limits and boundaries on the vastness of universal possibilities. and is reliant on interpretation with the possible miss-interpretation or purposeful twisting of words and intentions. The motions of the universe within natural law takes lifetimes to comprehend. Her task ahead is monumental.

Nothing would stop Charish from bringing motion to her passionate desire to balance self-governance with societies governance, to remind the populace who the real creators of government are, The Crown is nothing without the con-sent (mind sent) of the populace. Casting a spell of word salads capable of lighting a path towards our source creator, Charish became the purveyor of reason, the Sovereign Mother.

The University of the Quasaverse, the Crown's grooming school for leaders, adopted this new curriculum of natural law into the required courses for the gradual-ation, (never ending process of learning achievement), of the student leaders.

A gradual-ate of the University of the Quasaverse is guaranteed power over a portion of Queen Sparkle's realm of nothing. Well versed in Crown doctrines and dogmas, they are the validators of the Crowns authority, (script writers). The Crown programming is tapered by the wisdom of Natural Law, they could now become the servants of the populace instead of the rulers.

After the NARA prob craft retrieves Crys (our crystalline avatar construct) the Gateway Shuttle sets a course back to Mockery. The crew of the shuttle has added another member of the team. They continue to monitor the changes taking place because of the birth of the new sun 'Orbit,' the capture of Mockery into a sustainable orbit, the ripple of the time/space tapestry, then the re-formation of a new solar system within the Milky Way galaxy.

The trip back to Mockery gave the crew time to get to know Crys, Tap and Flow (original ponderer water avatar constructs) related to Crys, the first crystal construct. Crys quickly assimilated with his new surroundings, showing miraculous abilities that can change existence as we know it.

The Gateway crew helped Crys adapt as best they could, Tap and Flow were the most helpful. Crys was getting data from contact with this new reality he is experiencing. He is a natural receiver, reflector, absorber, and projector. Receiving the Pond entanglement was a major dump of information that started his struggle with incompleteness.

The experience of touching is a fascination for Crys, for eons the only touch he had was with the surroundings that were touching him. These surroundings never changed until the Gateway probe and the dream soul group arrived. Experiencing the heavens from a single perspective seamed so limiting now that he can move about to look at things from all points.

Touching, seeing, feeling, learning, hearing, moving about, and interacting are all hitting Crys in one big, long swoop. He moved about in what looked like a daze, touching everything and everyone.

The Pond consciousness entanglement has a unique effect on Crys, like a prism he can take a focused conscious light and project a colorful three-dimensional image of the stream of events. He could become a holographic projector, projecting any reality that any Ponderer was experiencing.

The holographic images that Crys projects have such precise detail that even miniscule features are easily recognized. Billions of story perspectives are available to access through Crys. He is a hit on movie night, although he became the first intergalactic holographic communication force, Holograms from the Entanglement Council could be studied by the crew of the Gateway shuttle.

From the Galactic Mystery Universities that teach the motions of the universe; co-motion is when we are in harmony with reality. The ebb and flow are synchronized like a dance, co-motion occurs when everything is in synchronization. Crys becomes like an orchestra leader creating unified co-motion to accomplish any task or challenge, his super quantum computing capacity is unlimited.

Crys uploads data at a pace never seen before, he will soon surpass both the Pond Consciousness and the NARA artificial intelligence.

With all the data streams that Crys is in-forming his spirit essence he is missing the experience of living and he lacks E-motion. He knows the meanings but has never experienced the feelings attached. The only e-motion Crys has felt is desire, with desire he found the will to become an avatar construct.

Uploading the histories that were guided by e-motions Crys did not fully comprehend the intentions behind a lot of action and reaction. Learning the description of love is not the same as feeling love. The E-motion spectrum runs from one extreme to the other, from desire to complacency, love to fear, happiness to sorrow. The e-motion spectrum includes feelings of all kinds that cause intention, leading to actions or inaction, that are governed by cause and effect.

When processing the governing of the aggregate/collective it is also ruled by e-motion. The mystery of e-motions that Crys faces has caused an e-motion of incompleteness, comprehending this chaotic force of e-motion causes a new e-motion within. Learning about A-motion masters has shown Crys that he may never achieve this higher state of being if he cannot feel e-motions, especially the e-motion of love.

Crys could see his home planet 'Plough' from the observation deck of the Gateway shuttle. He is separated from his fellow crystallite beings that he left behind, the entanglement that the Ponderers share with the Pond is not the same as the relationship Crys has with the Crystallites he left behind. The data he is downloading is not available to his crystal familiars, he must return someday to share his windfall of knowledge.

While looking back at planet Plough, Crys was washed by another e-motion of pensiveness, reflectiveness. What if he can never return? Maybe his e-motion range is larger that he believes. He is now experiencing loss, anxiousness, uncertainty, yearning, and maybe this is a form of love?

In just a brief period, mere seconds ago on a cosmic timestream, Crys was a stranded being in a remote reality, now he is a galactic being on adventures in the sea of space.

Cry is joined by Shawna while he was looking out the observation dome. Shawna shared her story of being a clone. The old girlfriend of the captain 'Seth,' was Shawna. She is now Shawna, complete with all of Shawna's memories, yet she was not Shawna. Her soul/spirit was retrieved from Seth's dreams then transferred into the vessel you see before you. All that makes her who she is, plus all she has yet to become.

Shawna became focused on a small object that appeared in her prereferral vision; out of the corner of her eyes she noticed it quickly getting closer. Her and Crys gave their full attention to the approaching object while alerting the rest of the crew to come look.

The only thing Crys was thinking was that these feelings must be excitement, curiosity. wonder, and anticipation. He gets a sense of gratefulness that he is experiencing this wide range of e-motions for the first time in his long existence. "Gratefulness," yet another new experience, this one seems to have some major power in the puzzle of existence.

After Crys returns from his mental drifting he joins the crew to observe the object that is now adjusting its course to match the Gateway's. Images appear in the minds of the crew, Crys projects these images with visual accuracy.

Greetings and introductions are pleasing, no harmful intent is felt, energy interpretation is an unspoken form of communication. Sensing intentions, also known as first impressions is instinctual to even a single cell.

These were obviously advanced beings with pure intent. Within moments a dialog was achieved.

The visitors spoke first; **we are the Plurals, there are many of us, the events taking place in this sector of the galaxy has brought about a lot of curiosity within the Quasaverse. The ripples in the sea space tapestry are lessening as they radiate outward. The reformation of the galaxy is continual. The birth of a star this massive is an event few have ever witnessed. The chaotic havoc that the galaxy faced by the rogue giant planet you call Mockery is brought into order. The time for healing is upon us all.**

Seth, the captain, spoke for the Gateway crew; **we are all part of a divine manifestation being orchestrated by a supreme consciousness that heals itself, seeking to thrive as all forms of life do. Mockery has no idea the galaxy was in any danger, there is a contained hidden solar system within the shell. This fractal universe is just now learning about the open sea of space and the infinity beyond their limited realm. We are returning to that realm to share the cosmic events they have unknowingly been part of.**

I am called Seth; I am the captain of this vessel. Welcome to our neighborhood, some of us are visitors here as well. This space shuttle you see is stranded here from across the galaxy. We have

established communication with our home but cannot return. Our home is the Sol solar system on the planet Earth.

The Plural spokesman replied; **they call me Duo, we are members of a galactic conglomerate of worlds called 'The Supreme Republic,' we have brought prosperity to all the worlds that join us. We are going to beam over a representative so we can get to know each other and invite you into the Republic. Please welcome Trio into your ranks.**

The Gateway shuttle crew will return with two new members. Trio made friends easily with everyone. He was able to help Crys orient to his environment while he did the same.

16

EVOLUTION VS. REVOLUTION

I-Motion and U-Motion

The Crowns capture of the remote territories in Mockery was not being accepted by much of the populace. There was a large percentage of beings that saw the seemingly benign intent of the Collective Crown as a slow path towards indentured slavery.

Pockets of discontent popped up in the populated regions, simple common-sense arguments assured the groups they were righteous in their beliefs. Raising arms against the Crown was always proved fruitless, the might of the Eternal Ember enforcers could not be overcome. They welcomed violence because that was something they could control, something that could be easily overwhelmed.

Examples of the Eternal Ember victories over violent uprisings were paraded in front of the remaining populace as warnings of the might they hold. The Embers were painted as heroes that protect the public from harmful intent. The Crowns coinage was introduced even forced on regions to accept this new way of trade.

The Collective Crown even orchestrated designed opposition, phycological operations, to show the futility of standing your ground, defending your space. These operations were planned, staged, acted out with the intent to teach a lesson of superiority that the Crown holds over the populace. These methods were justified with concern able rhetoric, rescuing a lost spirit, teaching a hard lesson, or protecting best interest.

Nomenclature, language, jargon is used as tools to create the illusion of superiority. The meanings of common words were given different definitions to entrap the innocent into the Crowns jurisdiction, making them second class citizens, like brutish pirates, the Crown enforcers drag everyone on to their virtual ship where they can control their destiny.

The Gateway shuttle is due to return to Mockery, the new crew members from far beyond will surely admire the iron hand that controls the populace. Queen Sparkle is not aware of the heavy hand bearing down on the beings she has sworn to protect. She issued an ordinance to bring everything within her kingdom of nothing under the umbrella of the Crown, to serve and protect. Overseeing the methods of achieving her mandate was carried out by her trusted military leader, Burney Smolder, who leads the legions of Eternal Embers.

Queen Sparkle believed that the survey exploration teams to map all corners of Mockery are on rescue missions to bring civilization to everyone. The teams are, expanding the influential strong arm of the Crown to every nook and cranny of planet Mockery.

The military might of the Eternal Embers was getting spread very thin, it became necessary to create mental prisons in the beings. Self-policing and imaginary onlookers, as in a panopticon, was introduced to populated areas to beef up the illusion of control.

King Zero and the University of the Quasaverse was teaching the tools and methods of building an Empire. The tools are being used to gain power by just a small fraction of the Collective Crown, using secrecy, this group of self-servers was planning a covert takeover of the Crown and Queen Sparkle.

It was clear that unrest was becoming prevalent among the populace, envy, and hatred of the immigrants from Ricochet/Yikes was being spread to further divide everyone into smaller fractions.

Scarcity was rumored to occur because of the new inhabitants when there is plenty for all.

Most of the unrest was going unnoticed by the Crown's inner circle surrounding Queen Sparkle and King Zero. Charish was the only one to see what was happening beneath their notice. She was in touch with the entourage that helped her on the world gauntlet games.

The narrative being broadcasted around the world focused on the negative events, diverting attention to fearful outcomes, psychopathic warfare to cause distrust. Charish counteracted this mental assault with messages of positive high vibrational quotes from her inner realm. "Love one another;" "trust natural law and creator;" "become one out of many, as many become one;" and many others that question the main narrative. Researching the maxims of law to use as guidelines to enlightenment.

The futility of having a revolution which puts you back at the beginning of the same path, did not ring true to Charish. It makes more sense to evolve beyond making the same mistakes, revolving over and over is fruitless.

Charish was a loved teacher at the University, her class started out by teaching the students who they are. **We are living through the apocalypse,** she would say; **how far along are you in realizing the apocalypse/the unveiling? Welcome to being a self-governing, self-determinate, self-aware, loving sovereign ingredient of the combined aggregate. You are the higher evolutionary hope for our reality.**

An unspoken battle for the minds of the aggregate began as soon as the Collective Crowns formation, even with the support of the Pond consciousness the free, self-aware beings questioning the results of centralizing into a hive civilization.

The global media broadcasting network run by HOW and WHY, the Poples of Mockery's loved celebrity superstars, supported the Collective Crown and all the ordinances, decrees, and declarations mandated by Queen Sparkle. The methods for enforcing these pronouncements are left to the discretions of the followers of the Crown.

Charish, the sovereign mother in Mockery, kept the peace as best she could. However the expansion of the Crowns realm has revealed an aggressive nature towards being the rulers. The persistence to be validated by others became a winner take all, free for all for the con/ minds of the populace.

From out of the confusion came a common workman Pople named 'Quasi,' he held the cosmic plunger of consciousness blockages, 'Swoosh.' The power of Swoosh was legendary. Tales of Swoosh were told to all the children in Mockery. The most recognized story is the clearing of 'Crapperton.' Crapperton was being flooded by I-motion dogmas.

I-motion, as you know, is the motions driven solely by self-interest. Out of balance I-motion causes a rush to the front, like crabs in a bucket. As soon as someone is getting ahead you must drag them back. Before long nothing moves forward, everything is stuck. It is a messy situation that can only be cleared by breaking apart the stopped-up beliefs, getting the minds flowing again is what the plunger does.

Quasi saved Crapperton from self-destruction, his arrival was in the nick of time. Just as things were considered hopeless, Quasi plunged the source of the blockage, self-centered became selfless-centered, freeing up the minds, a burst of U-motion, motions for others, allowing for O-motion or One-motion.

The sovereign mother Charish though that Quasi and Swoosh were just childhood stories until rumors of a mysterious Pople from the valley of Shamballa came to her from her trusted entourage. Quasi must be entangled with the Ponderers, while Flow and Tap are away in space with the Gateway crew, the Ponderer avatar construct 'Splash' was ambassador to the Crown. Splash was asked to do a sub-consciousness dive to find Quasi among the thousands of Ponderers existing in Shamballa.

Could Swoosh be the answer to the global unrest?

Beneath the notice of Queen Sparkle, Zero, and the Crowns inner circle, members of the Collective Crown started a vendetta against Charish, the sovereign mother. The smear campaign was the first step in this crusade. This movement to slander Charish would cause the populace to doubt the message being shared.

Bits of untrue in-formation were dripped to the global media. HOW and WHY released the news, the other networks followed suite without question. Accusations of brutal actions towards university students were whispered, rumors spread and the stories grew. The media validation cemented the accusation into the minds of the public.

Charish was found to be innocent of these accusations yet the damage was done. Step two of the affront was to frame Charish for a crime she did not commit, this would make the first accusations more believable. The barrage of deliberately false info masked as truth solidifies any doubt that Charish may not be the being most believe she is.

In all the assaults on Charish, she is found innocent although the seeds of doubt have been planted, the seeds were being nourished by persistent demeaning rhetoric.

Twisting the meaning of selected quotes to verify their imposing impressions of Charish was another tactic in this painted narrative. Even the concept of becoming sovereign was twisted into a self-serving, evil cult belief. The power of the microphone was outweighing the logic of the mind.

The abundant availability of the element Realium was having an unknown affect, those that realize that Realium is intentional magic, or the magic of intentions, were creating separate self-centered realities of their own. The miracle of manifestation should be in the hands of the wisest among the populace.

The unintentional effect of random reality manifestation, was causing con-flicks in the embroidery of society. This threatens the Collective Crown as well as the damage it was doing to the reputation of the sovereign mother Charish.

Society was changing at lightning speeds. Sixty percent of Mockery's populace are entangled with the Ponderers, this entanglement has the benefit of extended shared knowledge of the entire Pond consciousness network, the entanglement council, all the Pond's avatar constructs, and the NARA A.I. network. Even the entangled must access this unlimited library through intention, if they are distracted, they may never tap this resource.

Distraction from one's full potential is another ploy of the Crown traitors; unfocused intention creates chaos just as miss-focused intentions do. The campaign against Charish was really about beliefs, belief is the fuel for intentions. Influencing beliefs starts the shaping of society. Getting stuck on beliefs prevents advancement of knowledge and wisdom.

The cosmic plunger, 'Swoosh' is said to unblock the stuck beliefs, allowing the currents of information to flow freely, even the entangled get detached. Detachment allows a perspective of the tapestry, this  outside view of the entangled web, permits new in-form-ation, that form belief.

Just as the Gateway shuttle is set to re-enter the inner world of Mockery, the Entanglement  Council interrupted the planned return from their interstellar missions. It appears that yet another planet from an alternative solar system opposite the system Planet Plough came from. When this new planet reached the apex of their elliptical orbit, it got pulled into a new path around the  massive new star 'Orbit.' The new neighbor will circle close to Mockery and is predicted to become a moon around the gigantic planetoid Mockery.

The full impact of the resent celestial events has yet to be fully revealed. The crew agreed to investigate the approaching moon before returning to the womb of Mockery. This would add about two months to their mission and delay the introduction of Crys and Trio to the wonderlands of inner Mockery.

It took two weeks to reach the new moon, upon arrival it became clear that this stellar planet was not solid. The early probes revealed the moon surface was liquid, turbulent waves swashed about although a semi-solid plasma membrane kept the fluids contained.

The surface is also translucent, showing the movement of blobs beneath the exterior skin. The topography is in constant motion, the blobs are illuminating, different colors of illumination danced about in the currents within. A constant fog of cloud rose above the surface firmament making up the atmosphere of this amazing celestial wonder. The view from the deck of the Gateway displayed a liquid kaleidoscope, a marble in motion, magical, hypnotic beauty beyond imagination, moving through the sea of space.

The known natural laws of the Quasaverse should bring this Earth sized marble now named 'Wave,' into a large orbit around Mockery. Wave is just a speck compared to the gargantuan planetoid Mockery. The scale of this newly forming solar system is mind boggling.

A vibrational regularity was picked up by the sensers, there was a soothing harmony to the registered frequency being received and recorded. Flow, Tap, and Crys will easily endure even thrive in the atmosphere of Wave, a mission to the surface of Wave is planned, a shuttle pod is prepared for the round trip.

17

RESOLUTION

Multiple Me

This trip to Wave is the first mission that the newest crew members will undertake on their own. Flow, Tap, and Crys head to Wave with Crys at the helm. The progress Crys has made assimilating to his new environment is miraculous. His excitement for new adventures is contagious, the possibility for danger has not entered his inner realm of reality formation. The threat of danger is not anticipated and these are very capable beings.

The shuttle pod circled Wave a few times looking for a solid firmament to land the craft. Crys landed the pod like a master pilot on an island sloshing about on the turbulent surface of wave.

Tap remained on the shuttle pod as Flow and Cry stepped out into this wondrous environment. Flow instantly felt an overwhelming presence when contacting the surface, her entanglement with the milieu/setting was super charging her. The rush she felt was shared with the entire entangled network of trillions of beings across the galaxy.

All the Pond's consciousness was focused on what Flow was experiencing as she gathered herself together. Crys also felt the consciousness wave as a celestial entanglement was taking place with his companion Flow, all Ponderers and this cosmic planet.

The origin of Wave flashed in the visual cortex of the now captured hypnotized galactic entangled consciousness. Trillions of what we conceptualize as years ago, Wave was a single cell the size of a walnut. The source cell doubled every million years. Two, four, eight, sixteen, and so on. Wave has doubled in size every millennium sense celestial conception.

Wave is now one being, constructed of quadrillions of immortal replicas of itself. Wave is ready to double again soon, cosmic guidance is orchestrating a new path for this portion of the galaxy.

Up till now Wave has been kind of lonely with only himself to keep him intrigued. Learning how to live with himself has been his major obstacle. His jellylike consistency would at times snag a foreign object from the sea of space, merging with the planet like an ingredient in a soup.

The cosmic components of space are the nutrients for Wave, cosmic dust, small asteroid, comets, even moons have been devoured by Wave. Wave is a galactic clean up entity that will eventually be large enough to consume small planets.

The scattered remnants of the planet Ricochet/Yikes that fractured upon collision with Mockery have formed an asteroid belt that now circles Mockery in a wide orbit. These asteroids are a banquet for the multiple me planetoid being, Wave. This feast will fuel the coming split for Wave as he doubles in size in this millennium.

Wave would have eventually engulfed the smaller solar system he was exiting, the scale of everything was enormous in this new path, the Orbit solar system. Wave was once again a small fish in a large pond.

While the shared origin story played out to the entangled Ponderers, Wave was also downloading the story of the Pond and all the entangled network. It was at this point that the survival alarm bells went off for the away team of the shuttle pod, they were mere space dust to this celestial entity. The shuttle pod, Flow, Crys and Tap were in the grasp of this unintentional cosmic danger.

The away team landed on an asteroid that is being consumed by the multiple me being called Wave. Flow and Crys hurried back to the shuttle pod as Tap prepared for lift off. Lift off was being hindered by a creeping goo latching onto the landing skids. As the shuttle pod took off, the goo stretched, pulling them back to be consumed.

Fortunately Wave was grateful for the massive download from the Pond consciousness and was aware of the harm that his appetite was causing his new miniscule friends. The shuttle pod was allowed to escape.

A phycological link remained between Wave and the Ponderers as a whole planet became a new member of the Entanglement Council. Wave is re-named 'Quanto.' 'Meaning a currency of quantity,' is also called 'Quanto Wave,' the currents do cause waves. Quanto would never be alone/all-one in the same way again.

On the Star Ship Neuron the Entanglement Council headquarters was formed. It is becoming an intelligence network, NARA is the 'artificial intelligence,' the Ponderers are the 'elemental intelligence,' Jeb and Iam represent the 'interdimensional etherical intelligence.' Albert and the expanding soul group represent 'organic intelligence,' Crys represents 'mineral intelligence,' Quanto represents 'planetary intelligence.' Queen Sparkle and the Collective Crown represent the oxymoron 'political intelligence' or 'social intelligence.'

Evidence of 'cosmic intelligence' and 'celestial intelligence' is everywhere. Galactic self-preservation, a sign of intelligence, is proof of 'interstellar intelligence.' Communication with these higher forms of divine intelligence can be accomplished by A-Motion masters.

A-Motion divinity is accomplished by many in spurts, momentary brushes of heavenly insight have touched countless chosen beings to carry out planned blissful intention. The reformation of the galaxy is in constant flux, yet reigning in the destructive path of Mockery has been accomplished by intellectual intent.

Meetings of the Entanglement Council occurred weekly. Synchronizing time flow was like learning a new dialect, one week is measured in Earth rotations, the passive of time is measured differently by many concepts across the Quasaverse. One week for Quanto is just a bleep in time, an hour is a fraction of that bleep. Even in Mockery the concept of Earth time was hard to synchronize.

The combined intellect resolved the chronical synchronicity easily. In fact the Entanglement Council can blaze a new reality for the entire Quasaverse. Most of the meetings are held on the astral plane where distance and time are irrelevant. The ideal timestream for everything can now be navigated by analyzing the cones of probabilities for any major decisions.

Could the Entanglement Council be the intellect that orchestrated the timestream we are experiencing? Like a snake eating its tail, the Council could be the beginning and the end in the cycle of infinity. This is a popular theory among motion master students.

The main concerns of the Council now are the return of the vanished crew of the Gateway shuttle, the ripple in the tapestry of space caused by the birth of the infant sun Orbit, and the organization of a new solar system around Orbit. The unrest happening inside Mockery is a back burner concern for the Council. The long-term threat of the organic planet Quanto is also a possibility of little concern, as any risk is trillions of years away.

Most of the inhabitants of the Star Ship Neuron are now entangled with the Ponderer consciousness, Clog is free to wander about. The natural mindfulness upgrade that come with entanglement is recognized by everyone.

Everyone on Earth is fascinated by the stories coming from across the Milky Way galaxy. Re-enactments of these cosmic events draw crowds across the world.

Something that the Pople population feared is rearing its head inside Mockery. The rescue of Ricochet/Yikes beings went well despite the dangers of teleportation. Each Pople in Mockery has what they call sacred spots where they can safely teleport without fear of intermingling or inter-merging. Two objects cannot occupy the same space at the same time, porting into an occupied spot has unknown consequences and sometimes cause the passing of one or both the objects in the teleportation event.

Outlining and securing a sacred spot or zone is established after the first successful teleportation is complete. Each Pople has their own sacred spot, on Mockery these sacred zones are usually protected by safe cylindrical glass tubes to keep even the etherical beings from unintentional intermingling.

WOW established several sacred zones on planet Ricochet/Yikes after the first interplanetary teleportation with him and Wabble. There was no time to quarantine off a protected sanitized sacred zone like they had in Mockery. The brave Pople teleporters knew the risks yet faced these risks head on to save the lives of Ricochet populations.

What no one knew at the time was that Ricochet/Yikes had beings of conscious energy, not seen in our normal spectrums of sight. These etherical beings hitch hiked onto Pople teleportation on many of the interplanetary rescue trips. Many of the etherical energy beings attached themselves to other Ricochet beings for the trip. Not all of them realized what was going on with the surrounding chaos. This is where the etherical energy being we will call 'Shock,' was in the wrong place at the wrong time.

Shock found itself caught in a sacred teleporting zone just as the Pople called WHUH popped in from Mockery. Shock and WHUH intermingled without WHUH even being aware of any internal changes. A emergence of two energies, one physical and the other etherical. Shock went unconscious when WHUH popped into the time/space where it was occupying. The mergence was instantaneous.

WHUH made many interplanetary teleportation trips with the stowaway Shock before the collision event knocked Mockery on the path to salvation. WHUH has long ago finished his last trip when he began having another voice inside his mind. At first the voice sounded groggy as if waking from a long slumber. Soon, the voice became stronger, WHUH began seeing other etherical beings everywhere and he was not sure what was going on within.

Strange visions and voices within made WHUH think he had a terminal illness, he sought help wherever he could. His unusual behavior made him stick out when around others.

Finally an ancient wise Pople diagnosed WHUH with 'inter-mergence,' this has not occurred in Mockery for many generations. Inter-mergence is not like entanglement, entanglement is an upgrade to one's self, inter-mergence is two or more separate entities occupying the same physical vessel.

WHUH was advised to get to know and love his mind mate, otherwise there would be an internal battle that may destroy both the host and the inhabitant. WHUH named his inner companion 'Shock' because of the feelings he had struggling with his new circumstances; Shock loved his new designation.

Shock gave WHUH new abilities that amazed his fellow Poples, flight, prophetic visions, pulse beams of pure energy, access to parallel realms, intangibility, and invisibility. He became unsure of his teleporting ability.

Shock and WHUH would have internal scuffles that amused onlookers who watched. He/they bolted to and frow, up and down, speaking back and forth in unknown dialects, one would think he/they were silly crazed. In sanity was in constant turmoil.

WHUH's internal mayhem mimicked the unrest happening between the populace of Mockery and the power-hungry faction threatening the Collective Crown. The resolution to both struggles is the same, only love and compromise will peacefully resolve the pandemonium.

18

CELEBRATIONS

Solutions

Excitement grew as the Gateway shuttle returned inside Mockery. Celebrations were planned around the world with the main event being held on the University of the Quasaverse campus. Global media set up to cover this welcome back party. Campus groups united for the celebration preparations; higher education encouraged collaboration for common goals. This uniting was a lesson designed by Charish, the Sovereign Mother in Mockery.

The celebrations would kick off with a parade from the Gateway shuttle landing site through the pathways of the university campus ending at the gaming stadium where the party will begin. The celebrations are broadcasted globally, the excitement is real, everyone is involved as a participant or an observer.

Ballons, floats, banners, graffiti, musicians, plays, and creative works all held a sentimental place in the festivities. The new monetary system of exchange was now issuing fiber paper tokens as the accepted means of conversion. The Collective Crown treasury is producing this paper money for fractions of the declared value.

These celebrations are the event needed to introduce the new currency. All attendees must make purchases with the new moneys or do without. A system of easy exchange was set up where valuables are exchanged for paper dollars that allow you to purchase other values. Paper is much easier to carry around, coins and other values may be cumbersome. An exchange fee/tax is charged on every transaction paying the Collective Crown treasury for providing this new system.

The news about the birth of infant sun Orbit is still fresh in the information network. Stories about planet Plough, the Plural Supreme Republic, and the organic planet Quanto marveled everyone. Expectations of meeting the outworlders Crys and Trio was growing as the stories spread.

The Gateway shuttle landed smoothly; the crew stepped out as a large crowd cheered. Seth stepped up to the megaphone to thank and inform the populace.

The universe around us is wonderous; Seth spoke with excitement; **we have witnessed marvels of the imagination. A balancing of reality is taking place as we speak. Just outside the world that you know, an infinite sea of space extends in every direction. Within this vast expanse is unlimited miracles we are part of. The birth of the infant sun 'Orbit' has heralded in a new millennium for this portion of the galaxy, bringing this world into a family of celestial neighbors that will thrive, healing everything around.**

We now have the greatest assemblage of knowledge ever achieved, access to this knowledge is available to all willing to search. The never-ending curving path all lead to our source creator. Come with us as we share the adventures just around your corner.

Working with us, hand in hand, is the Entanglement Council, based on a Star Ship across the galaxy in our home solar system Sol. Together we have the greatest analytical, diagnostic, scientific problem solvers ever gathered. At the spearhead of this collection is a family soul group we are proud to call friends, Albert Jennings and his talented group have experienced reality, soaking up source formation in astounding ways.

From the planet Plough we have a new ally companion 'Crys,' who is on a trail of discovery, just as we all are. He travels this path in wonderment, at a rate of input beyond contemplation. Next, we will introduce a fellow explorer from the Plurals Supreme Republic, a galactic society now sharing our agreed reality. 'Trio,' is re-presenting our cosmic numeric neighbors, the Plurals. Mathematics is the shared language of all consciousness; Trio is the magical number of validations.

Just outside your terraformed crust is a being the size of one of your moons, circling this world, cleaning the open sea of space surrounding plant Mockery. This ancient being was called Wave at first but now goes by the designation 'Quanto.' Quanto is the newest member of the Entanglement Council who are working on benefits for all.

Thank you for this magical reception, the crew of the Gateway shuttle have awaited our return with apprehensive excitement for days.

The Gateway crew entered an open air floating vehicle and gave the parade wave to all the gathered onlookers. The roadway had beings from all corners of Mockery eager to see the heroic space explorers. The parade caravan entered the stadium where the Collective Crown royalty awaited to greet the returned crew.

Queen Sparkle was the first to greet the crew and welcome them back to Mockery, Charish, the sovereign mother and King Zero were by her side. Sparkle's speech addressed the accomplishments of the society the Collective Crown was making; **welcome back, as you can see, the whole globe is here in one form or another for your return and to meet your new crew members. While you were away, Mockery has advanced in many ways, there are teams of explorers searching every corner of Mockery, discovering lost societies to join Crowns beneficial reign.**

The Crown treasury is now printing currency in mass production to bring wealth to every citizen of the Crown, the value of the Crown coins has risen as they become collectables and fade out of circulation. All exchanges will take place using the Crown money system. The Crown is granting shared ownership to loyal

patrons to the Collective. Everything falls under the protective umbrella of the Crowns mighty grip.

Education is now available to all; the assigned curriculum will patronize the student to the Collective Crown. The best and brightest of the students will be granted scholarships to the University of the Quasaverse and possibly move into positions within the ruling Collective Crown inner circles where they will thrive. We are molding and shaping the future of Mockery in the image of our galactic visitors' tutorials.

The Crown is a member of an intergalactic organization called the Entanglement Council. The Entanglement Council is provided by the Pond consciousness and in constant contact with beings from a world called 'Earth.' Earth is the home world of the Gateway shuttle visitors that have enriched our world and saved this whole interstellar region of outer space.

Our greatest scientist and engineers are working on a cosmic portal bridge to return our visitors to their home solar system and begin trade between our vast empires. The combined knowledge of three interstellar empires, the collective intelligence of our natural existence is at our fingertips.

The Collective Crown and I, your Queen Sparkle's accomplishments are numerous, our potential is infinite.

Queen Sparkle gave the megaphone over to Zero who started his rhetoric with a sarcastic joke; **after today's activities you all need to return to your prisons that you are creating with the help of the Collective Crown.** No one laughed so he did not skip a beat; **your capitulation is greatly appreciated and makes it possible for us to rule over you.**

It was clear that no one shared Zero's humor, he thinks the neutering of society is a humorous necessity to creating an empire plantation. Zero continued; **bwaa ha, ha, my friends, your evil captures love you, have fun in your slavery, we all serve someone or something, you may as well serve your Queen Sparkle. The crown will reward you for your willing surrender and punish all those who oppose the will of the Crown. Just kidding!! Or am I?**

Sparkle grinned an impish smile as she inwardly giggled at Zeros' awkward attempt at levity. Zero was her mentor and could not do or say anything wrong.

After a contemplated pause, Zero continued; **I will stop highlighting the rights you all must give up to the collective and let you know you do not have to give up any of your natural rights if you know who you are, but you need to figure that out yourself. The Collective Crown is there for those who do not discover their self-worth, we are here to milk you of your worth. Just kidding!! Or am I?**

No one but Zero thought he was funny, this tickled Zero even more, with a wink and a smile he continued; **OK, ok, ok, so, you find out who you are, you are the life force of a physical vessel that shares your reality with a stew of energy vessels, you are a co-creator of your reality. All your creations belong to the crown because you are within the crown's realm. Just Kidding!! Or am I?**

You determine who you are and where you fit into the aggregate surrounding you. You are who you are because of your environment, the crown is the main co-creator of the shared reality that formed your inner dialog you mistake as you. What you learn is just data that you gather to enable you to live and possible thrive in your surroundings. This data is not you; you are the center of a unique universe that is in a realm of many universes we call the Quasaverse.

The purpose for this rant on this monumental occasion is to settle the unrest being stirred up among the populace. The trust you may or may not hold towards the Collective Crown is a personal choice. You must be your own governor between you and your outer realm. You are in charge, if you advisor is love, you will find your purpose.

Everything has a value, a cost, a price, a purpose, and a source of energy. You determine all these things, do not sale yourself cheap or limit your worth, yet recognize the value, cost, price, purpose, and energy around you. Our new money system is just a tool of exchange, when using this tool with love, everyone can thrive. If you use this tool with malice, it will eventually destroy you and those around you.

Zero felt like he was admonishing himself by revealing the truth to the populace, he has a bit of a guilt complex as he is the catalyst that created the Collective Crown. Washing his hands of any decisions anyone would make, will ease his karma. He continued; **remain in control of your buying and spending, your expansion and contraction. Your energy can circulate, helping everyone, or it can support a monster that will eventually consume you.**

The brightest among you may have what it takes to attend the University of the Quasaverse, where you can rule your own reality with the wisdom of the gods and goddesses you are.

I hope you can see the whole puzzle picture, rest easy but be diligent, go forward with love.

Welcome back the explorers from the Gateway Shuttle, my crewmates, and extra-terrestrial visitors from just beyond your inner world of Mockery.

Let me re-introduce my friend from beyond, 'Clipper' the scientist that has helped orchestrate the events that have saved an entire solar system. Give him a warm welcome.

Clipper stepped up to the megaphone focused on presenting the plans. Construction of star portals are underway, an interstellar sterile controlled environment that connects two distinct spots in time/space; **we have audio contact with the Gateway shuttle home planet Earth.** Clipper started out; **this is key to making the impossible, possible. Interstellar trade will bring about a new age for everyone.**

Those opening lines Clipper started off with will be remembered for a long time as his magical presentation appeared in the stadium, a holographic image of the proposed Star Port showed technology, science, engineering, magic, wonder, and potential, lit up the air for the onlookers.

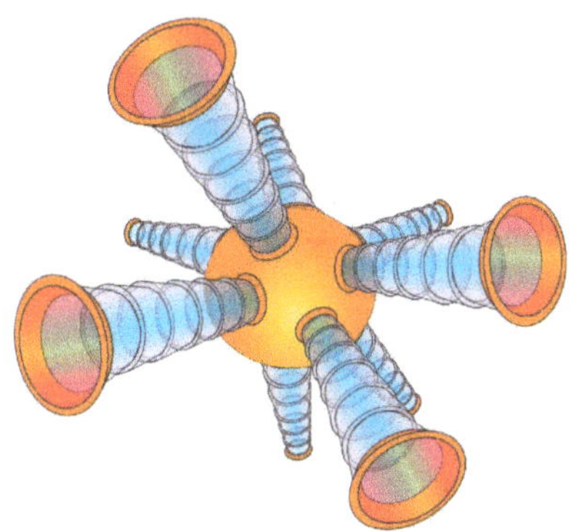

Clipper took advantage of this "wow' moment stating; **when you see the resources we have within our grasp, you will see that this is an easily obtainable project.**

Our NARA mini bots have endless possibilities, they can replicate into task-oriented purposes. Miner bots, builder bots, mover bots, replicator bots, and so on. The building blocks are present everywhere in the sea of outer space.

NARA replicating bots have been working in your outer space for days now, the intention blueprint is downloaded into NARA's mainframe in both locations of Mockery and Earth. The replication rate is amazingly fast, with the magic number sixty-four as turning point in the new bot's existence. The block of sixty-four choose their own purpose at this magic number and perform as one, all are equipped with NARA main frame connection but the designation is a group choice.

The entire structure will be a large NARA space port made of billions of NARA bots with singular purposes. The NARA main intelligence shares the imaginative visions that guide this massive project, work at both ports should take one Earth year before first porting can take place and The Gateway shuttle can finally return home. The Portal station will have eight port chambers and is being named the 'Octaport.'

The teleporters existing on Earth work on molecular breakdown then reconstruction, living biological matter is never ported to avoid the massive data needed in rematerializing with possible miss-information. The new technology teleports using vibrational frequencies, going, and receiving intentional commands, Realium reality manipulators, and pocket universes. The porting is nearly instantaneous, there is a milli-second in the pocket dimension.

The interstellar teleport station will be centered by a welcome center with orientation, a galactic shopping mall, and gift center. Shuttles like The Gateway shuttle will transport to neighboring planets to experience the wonders of source creation.

Keep this visual goal in your frontal quartet as it will surely aid in the manifestation of this intended project. Thank you for your undivided attention, blessings to everyone. With that, Clipper stepped down from the speaker podium waving to the cameras and crowd.

Celebrations continued for many hours.

19

INTERGALACTIC ENGINEERING

Answers Within

Construction of the Octaport continued earnestly on Earth and Mockery. The Plurals brought a lot of help to the NARA construction bots, the mining bots needed raw material. The Plurals hauled giant remnants from the destroyed planet Ricochet/Yikes orbiting Mockery to the building site. They helped with the processes of turning the raw material into an indestructible material like Plexi glass with wonderous properties necessary for withstanding the rigors of the sea of outer-space.

The immigrant beings from Ricochet/Yikes can someday soon return to a reincarnation of their home planet, the cycle of life transforms with new purpose. The Plurals shared this process of making this space enduring material with the sister construction site taking place near the Star Ship Neuron in the Sol solar system.

Co-operation between the two building sites was orchestrated by the Entanglement Council. The gathered intelligence of the all one source is contributing to the design's operational capabilities of these massive projects. The designs cater to beings of many origins.

Mankind is working hand in hand with cosmic entities, alien beings, inter-dimensional immortals, and the greatest technologies. Some believe man was at the pentacle of our civilization and we are due to a downward swing on the pendulum of life, while the dreamers feel we are at the beginning of a path that only leads even greater possibilities. The best is getting better and better.

The building techniques, engineering feats, and design manifestation are streamlined into a musical flow, using sound and frequency in ways only a genius mind would comprehend. They say there is no sound in space, sound is vibration, vibration is energy, frequency creates and shape matter. Like how Albert's daughter Penny matches the frequency to create her bubble creations, mankind is learning how to create geometric shapes for building by matching the tones and frequency of the desired geometric shape. Harmonic resonance shapes the indestructible crystalized Plexiglass tube that make up the humongous port chambers.

The NARA builder bots duplicated the Gateway shuttle to serve as a tour guide into outer space and out of the inner world of Mockery. Another shuttle was built to work as meteor haulers bringing material to the building site.

Members of the original Gateway shuttle crew took on new roles in training the new crews manning the shuttles being built. Peep taught and trained the newly formed galactic force, Clipper taught courses in science and engineering. Jinn did nothing as usual, yet things happened around him.

Seth and Shawna continued running missions on the Gateway shuttle. Flow, Tap, WOW, Crys, Trio, and Wabble have become the crew on the new missions. This brings us to the next milestone in this story, the Supreme Republic that the Plurals are the leading member, is needing help on a colony world in a nearby solar system.

This was a big colony of a billion souls that had a devastating storm that nearly wiped them out. The abundance in Mockery was now being shared on a galactic scale sparking opportunities for entrepreneurs who wish to help and prosper. A large care package was gathered that filled the Gateway shuttle storage to its limits. A six-week round trip aid mission takes off on an undertaking of passionate intent.

The Plurals call this colony planet 'Halo.' Halo is a hard light world, a natural illumination was present in every grain of sand, every rock, every plant held a self-contained light, with just the right amount of dark to show shape and texture. A small amount of Halo sand can illuminate a large room forever, the color spectrum is stretched with dazzling shades not seen by our normal vision.

The indigenous beings on Halo are holographic light beings that can control their density. They can also control the brightness or dimness of their luminosity, when dimmed down they are invisible and more tangible.

The colonizers are like the Plurals and are the one in most need of aid. The storm wiped out the shelters they inhabited, the fields of planted nutrition were destroyed, the survivors gathered in small groups finding whatever they could to get by.

The Indigenous 'Haloids' had a different set of needs to get sustenance. They have thrived in the environment on Halo which is almost toxic to the colonizers, the shelters protected them from the harsh surroundings but also provided the colonizers with what they needed. The remaining resources were quickly being depleted.

The colonizers harvested a mineral on Halo that was harmful to the Haloids, so there was a symbiotic tolerant relationship between the two groups. Unfortunately, however much the two groups relied on each other, the Haloids were of no help in this situation. The only help they could provide was temporary shelter, the other necessary nutrients for the colonizers were now in limited supply.

The Plurals mother ship would also send a care package but the Gateway was providing NARA technology in their rescue bundle, this was an opportunity to advance relations between Mockery, the Gateway shuttle, and the Supreme Republic.

This mission would soon take a wide turn, the Gateway sent an advance pod while orbiting Halo with Flow, a NARA probe, and Crys. The Pod landed near a temporary housing site where many the colonizers that survived the storm gathered.

Flow exited the Pod to meet with the Haloids, but stayed away from the Colonizers to avoid unintentional entanglement; the Haloids seemed to be immune to the Ponderers entanglement although Flow felt a bond with them. There is one Haloid that Flow was drawn to, finding him among the Haloid populace was the challenge. The Haloids surrounded Flow in curiosity as she walked among them.

As Flow got close to her mysterious attraction she felt a tingling sensation, like a series of mild jolts, or a continual buzz. The vibrations were causing Flow to unvoluntary shape shift, beautiful geometric shapes formed a grand layer of shimmering texture that danced on her outer hard water skin. The illuminations around her reflected like a many faceted sparkling diamonds, as she moved, she glistened like shimmering moonlight on a rippling lake.

It was clear who Flow was drawn to, when she got in front of him, she completed her metamorphosis. The Haloid was just as surprised, before him was this angelic alien being who just went through a remarkable transformation. All eyes were on Flow as she reached out for the hand of her kindred spirit from another world.

For the first few moments, Flow's speaking sounded like gibberish, distinct sounds with no apparent meanings. As she spoke her words gained meaning and the Haloids began to comprehend her verbal melody; **I am known as Flow, we are from planet Mockery and planet Plough. Some of us are from across the galaxy, a planet called Earth. We are here to help the Colonizers on your world.**

The Haloid responded saying; **I answer to the audible 'Bright,' welcome. We call our home 'Halo,' do you plan on staying? We will do what we can to make you feel welcome.**

The greetings are brief, as to everyone's amazement, Flow was still going through an alteration, her belly was growing and glowing.

Flow's transformation gave her gossamer butterfly wings, she also felt something growing inside her, Flow was with child. New life was forming inside her from the vibrational barrage she felt while approaching Bright. This new life was growing at a rapid rate. A cosmic child of inter specie origins was about to grace our universe.

This celestial conception was foretold in the legends of the Haloid beings, the story goes; an alien angelic being from the stars would someday come to Halo and bring about the enlightened savior.

The gathered Haloid crowd held witness as Flow's child grew inside her before their eyes, Bright was able to sooth Flow as she had a small panic attack. Nothing like this has ever occurred throughout the Pond consciousness billions of years existence. The entangled all felt Flows range of e-motions, all the Ponderers, the entanglement council, across the galaxy, the entire entangled pond ethereal web, will share in the birthing of the transcendent child of the Quasaverse.

Flow returned to the Gateway pod with Bright. Crys and the NARA probe had made arrangement for the Colonizers to receive their care package, then returned to the pod as well. The urgency of Flow's miracle was not going to slow the action to bring relief to the Colonizers.

The NARA probe switched into replicate mode as a package drop from the Gateway shuttle is dropped where it is needed most. This would be an extended stay on Halo for the Gateway shuttle away team.

NARA's replicators had a new task to choose, as a temporary shelter is needed to house the away team and prepare for the birthing of the celestial baby.

This is the most anticipated event in the Quasaverse, at any moment a new life form will enter prime reality. Albert's soul group are attending the birthing event as astral photon projections, they will be a great asset if anything goes astray.

Flow is glowing as the time gets close for her baby to enter. The harmonics heard when Flow and Bright first met have been added to musical overture's being played to the fetus growing inside Flow. There is a telepathic connection between Flow and the baby, they agreed on the name, 'Aqua Light.'

As Aqua was forming a feminine vessel that can feel and sense. Each feeling being sensed was forming e-motion within her, Flow was careful to provide the highest frequencies for Aqua's early development. Aqua will be entering a reality that is full of an unlimited spectrum of energy frequencies, she will need the greatest love regularities to grow strong.

With the advantage of being entangled with over a billion souls and the memory of the Ponds millennial existence, Aqua will be born with more knowledge than most acquire in an entire lifetime. They say that it takes a village to raise a child, this child is entangled with the village.

The Haloids legends speak about their chosen one being born on Halo, but will live among the stars with godlike beings for thirty years before returning to Halo where she will lead the world into a new age of peace and prosperity.

From far and wide the shamans of Halo began a pilgrimage to the Gateway pod with the saviors birthing site. They brought with them the items they felt would enrich the child of the Quasaverse, gold, diamonds, herbs, seeds, realium, technologies, music, art, every value one can think of, yet there was no Collective Crown coins or paper currency. What held value to the beings was just stuff to Aqua, Bright, and Flow, although love and gratitude was shared with all.

Being adorned with positive vibrations is the greatest gift to a developing entity. The formation of every cell is bathed in adornment. The validation of existence is the fuel for matter creation, a staple for being.

The Colonizers are well on their way to becoming self-sustainable again as the birthing day approaches.

20

NEAR COMPLETION

Innocent Intelligence

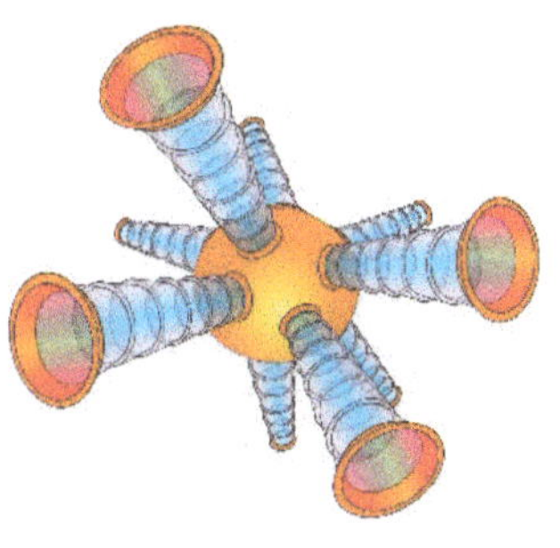

Construction on the inter-galactic Octa-ports was progressing nicely. In just a few months the preparation stages were operating like a well-orchestrated chorus, manufactured material was getting positioned for assembly. NARA worker bots moved about with purposeful intent; the completed puzzle picture was ingrained in their programing.

NARA bots were also in full production, this will enhance the productivity of the project. The Star Ship Neuron NARA bots are being re-purposed towards Port construction.

Teleportation has been a technology on Earth for over twenty years, the ports on Earth are being revamped as the technology is upgraded with the added element Realium. Realium has been discovered on Mars as well as the existing mine on the moon of Titan. The ancient Martians must have been aware of the magical properties of Realium

Realium has been proved to be an intention intensifier, the new technology is centered around intention manifestation. Intention centers are being set up at all the Tela-Ports. Meditating with an intentional focus, aligning with the frequencies of that intention is key to successful intergalactic teleportation. Both the sender and the receiver need to be focused on the intentions.

Navigating the time/space ocean is a perplexing difficulty, the constant motion of everything means you must anticipate location using both time and space, or have a transponder pinpointing locations. Intention centers are the transponders for the new teleportation ports.

Imagine being able to create reality just by using focused intentions, your job/purpose/essence is being an intention conduit for part of your day. The universe matches your intentions so you are a validator for reality in your natural state.

The Orbit, Mockery Octa-Port was a bit behind the Sol Earth site. The Gateway shuttle was still away on Halo, they had the help of the Supreme Republic and the elements needed for material production was readily available, so things should progress nicely. Creating NARA task bots capable of working in the sea of space was step one.

Clipper was leading the NARA bot production, teaching the beings of Mockery new technologies and creating professional careers never realized in Mockery before. The Crown treasury was financing the whole project using paper currencies backed by the future sweat equity of the beings in Mockery. This makes the beings of Mockery the grantors of the creation.

The construction of the Octa-Port has been a great unifier in Mockery, the grand scale of the project is dazzling, attractive to the curious mind. There is an awakening of an entire world to the wonder of the vast Quasaverse, recently a world sheltered by a limited perspective, living in a cosmic womb with no knowledge of the what lies beyond. Now they are part of an intergalactic symphony in the making.

The first duplicate of the Gateway shuttle was complete, it is called 'The Endeavor,' the crew is being chosen by Peep. Charish has been asked to captain the new space shuttle, with Quasi as first mate. The volunteers for crew members are going through a vigorous training that will surely produce the cream of the crop. The crew should have at least one Pople teleporter, one Ponderer, and one Eternal Ember.

The Sol Earth site had many resources already being produced; their network was already in place.

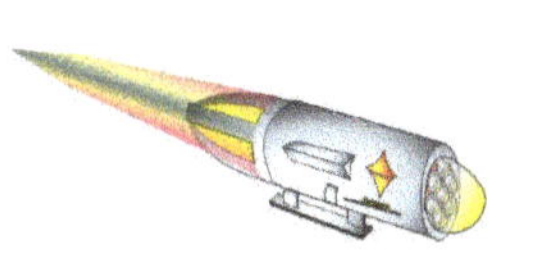

The time for the birth of Aqua was rapidly approaching, a small community has gathered for the anticipated event. The Entanglement council has information from the akashic records provided by Zeb and Iam, a multidimensional ancient spirit is said to be reanimating in this three-dimensional reality as the child Aqua. This spirit is said to be the oldest recorded being in the Quasaverse, reanimated on billions of worlds in the past as the bringer of illumination. The bringer has gone by many names throughout eternity. Aqua will **not** have the memories of these past lives when she is born, forgetfulness is a price for reanimation. Remembering can be achieved with focused intent.

Aqua will be born with the consciousness, the memories of the Pond, the Ponderers, the Entangled and the loving vibrations of the Haloids gathered.

Myra will be Flow's mid-wife as an astral projection, coaching Crys in the birthing. This is not like any birthing ever in existence, Myra's essence ability to heal any kind of dis-ease makes her the natural choice for this miracle task. Myra is also entangled with the Ponderers, so she will have an added connection to the miraculous birthing event.

With everything going on around Flow, the birth was a very private affair. The birth happened quickly, it was almost instantaneous, like a teleportation, Aqua went from Flows' belly and into her arms. Myra

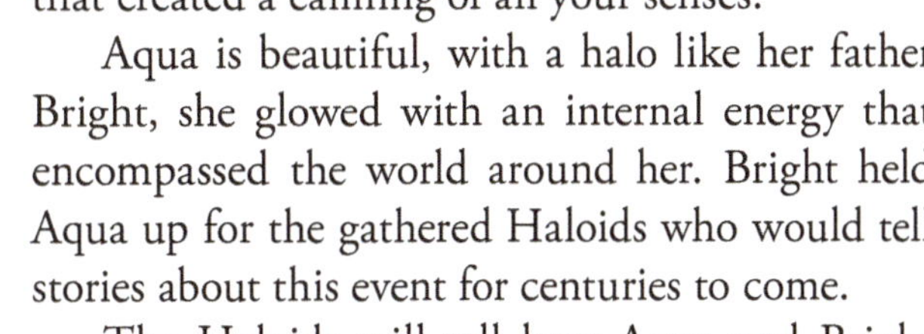

could feel the harmony of wellness, a vibration that created a calming of all your senses.

Aqua is beautiful, with a halo like her father Bright, she glowed with an internal energy that encompassed the world around her. Bright held Aqua up for the gathered Haloids who would tell stories about this event for centuries to come.

The Haloids will tell how Aqua and Bright entered a shiny craft that lifted them up to the stars above, leaving them with the knowledge that Aqua will return on many occasions to come.

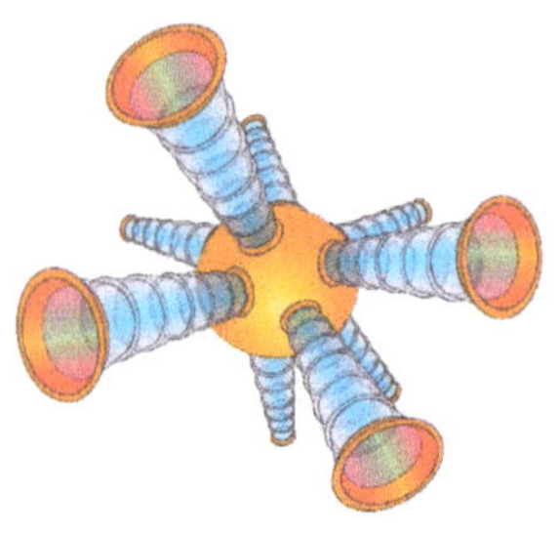

The Gateway away pod returned to the Gateway shuttle with both Bright and Aqua returning with them, the mission to aid the Colonizers was complete and it was time to return to help with the Octa-port project and get the Gateway shuttle back home.

Progress on the Octa-port was moving along at an alarming rate, when the Gateway shuttle got back it was taking shape. The central hub had all eight ports attached. Most of the work is internal now. The scale of the ports is amazing, a massive starship could easily port into any one of them. The Gateway shuttle is a speck in comparison.

All of Mockery awaited the chance to meet baby Aqua. Flow is equally a celebrity as the first and only ever Ponderer mother. Bright was a minor curiosity but anticipation still ran at a high frequency. This was the first interplanetary family. The welcome wagon was not as grand as previous celebrations, the Gateway was greeted by the world news broadcasters. Every tele-viewer was tuned into the broadcast.

Queen Sparkle was privately harboring a cringe of jealousy about the world-wide popularity of the family. She struggled with the notion to start a smear campaign to turn the world against them. She has always struggled with her petty tirades, but this one tested her resolve. This child is prophesized to become queen of the Orbit solar system, which will place Sparkle and the Collected Crown under the domain of baby Aqua. Sparkle's realm of nothing will end up with nothing.

Sparkle did overcome her obsession with Charish, the champion of the gauntlet games, and the sovereign mother. Aqua was a bigger threat to Sparkles rule over Mockery, she would let this imaginary threat fester her spirit for days before coming to grips with any possible outcome for the future. She decided instead to meet with Flow, Bright and baby Aqua and rise above these insecurities.

Sparkle gathered the Royal Court, the Collective Council, and the Gateway crew, to a feast at the Imperial Plantation to greet and honor the arrival of baby Aqua into this shared reality. The grand ballroom is party ready, the best musical talent in Mockery was scheduled for the occasion.

The red carpet was rolled out for the guests, exotic landscaping graced the entrance, everything was pristine. Each arrival was announced for all to hear, this was a grand affair that has never been imagined in Mockery before.

Trumpets blow with the arrival of the guest of honors. Flower pedals were spread on the path in front of them as they walked, angelic fairies like Sparkle herself, dropped the pedals that magickly appeared out of their tiny hands as they flew. Sparkles kindred beings all loved their Queen, their control of the amazing element Realium is unmatched.

The original crew of the Gateway shuttle would be together again for the first time since the Orbit celebration. Years have passed and nothing is the same. They were the catalyst for most of this change. No one knew the path before they started walking it, Zero's clever ruse when they arrived has blossomed into a grand empire with enormous potential.

Eternal Embers hung still in the air lighting the way through the massive mansion, the Embers are the most self-disciplined beings in Mockery and they are loyal to their Queen Sparkle.

Various Ponderers represented the Pond were there to see this miraculous mother and child, The Ponds Ponderer avatars have taken many preferred shapes, individuality is a Ponderer fetish, being tied to a cosmic consciousness has its advantages but self-awareness, self-preservation, and self-determination were badges of pride.

The largest attendees were the Poples, HOW and WHY were there to cover the story for their broadcast station, and see WOW. The Pople surveyors that braved the exploration of the world attended as governors of the newly discovered or rediscovered pocket civilizations in Mockery. Decorated Pople teleporters, including the merged WHUH/Shock hero who reminded everyone the dangers and possibilities of teleportation.

Ricochet/Yikes refugees' representatives reportable roamed the ranks of the roster. Wabble willingly wiggled his way within the wishing wonder.

The feast was spread out on a long pristinely decorated table, each species had their own dietary preferences, there was something for everyone. The banquet ended as the dance floor populated.

Once again, the baby Aqua was adorned with gifts of cherished valuables from all corners of Mockery. Aqua slept through most of the celebrations, unattached almost unaware of the adornment. She was unintentionally like a sponge soaking up her surroundings. The positive energy was reverberated back to the crowd as a feeling of completeness.

21

HOMEWARD BOUND

Interstellar Web

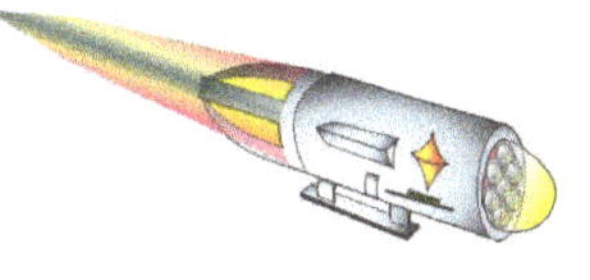

The Octa-Port was ready for testing, the infrastructure on both locations was complete. The first test is non-organic, an empty vessel is to be teleported from the Sol Earth port to the Mockery port and back.

Specific intentions are intoned in the intention centers. Envisioning the intention as if it has already occurred is a paramount step, with the sender visualizing the object and the destination port while the receiver visualize the object in their port. The test port was instantaneous, a detailed inspection of the cargo was done before sending the cargo back to the first port across the galaxy. The teleport back had a brave volunteer to test the safety, once again Wabble took this risk.

Testing the limits of the powers of intentions and manifestation is pushing the envelope of believability. The ability to believe makes one qualified to become an intention master.

The test went smoothly, a complete success. The return trip for the vanished Gateway shuttle was now possible. Zero and Clipper will choose to stay behind as many choose to join the crew and go with the Gateway. Flow, Bright, Crys, baby Aqua, WOW, Tap, Wabble, and Quasi will become crew members on a permanent basis as well as galactic celebrities.

The return trip is planned when the Gateway shuttle returns from its last local mission. Before they leave, they will return into Mockery to plan the next path for this network of cosmic players. The possibilities are endless. but need to be taken one step at a time.

The Gateway shuttle entered Mockery and landed at their first landing site. A platoon of Eternal Ember soldiers met them when they land and escorted the crew to Queen Sparkle, where she was waiting with the royal court. A meeting with the entanglement council is scheduled, most of the attendees are there as remote viewer astral projections.

Expansion of the Octa-port network is the agenda for the meeting. Local galaxies have been visited by remote viewers for decades now where new life and endless natural resources are available. The technologies to visit these places physically is now readily available once a port is in place. The plans are to send NARA un-manned crafts out to all directions with single ports and intention centers to set up a transporting network of interstellar proportions.

Albert and his soul group have developed an intention recorder that stores the energy, feelings, beliefs, vibrations, frequencies, and purpose of an intention into a crystal sphere that can be activated remotely. These intention spheres, 'crystal balls,' can capture and store then relieve intentions, the limit is that they are good for one use only, once the intention is dispersed it cannot be re-captured. They will be able to kick start a remote port with an intention sphere.

The expansion would take place from three regions, the Sol Earth solar system, the Orbit Mockery system, and the Plurals Supreme Republic's original home solar system. A port was already being set in the Plural's home solar system.

There are over five thousand remote locations chosen for port locations, some are in the Andromeda galaxy and will not be activated for several years. The expansion will take time but will become the greatest artificial interstellar transportation network ever conceived, by man, with the Octa- ports being the centers of the cosmic web being created.

Albert has visioned the network in completion, he knows that to maintain positive value to this expansive network, the E-motion of love must be the only key that can activate any port intention sphere. Low vibrational harmful intents will shut down any port instantly, making them in-operatable. One of the best ways to spread love is to not allow the lower motions of the Quasaverse to infect and spread.

Myra, now considered the celestial healer, has taken extra precaution to stop the spread of harmful intentions that bring a dis-ease that infects reality. The wellness of everything is within our grasp, treating the malignancies that crop up with the love vibration, is the cure needed. The past behaviors that cause war, strife, cruelty, selfishness, jealousy, maliciousness, greed, and other negative E-motions, are shamed, ridiculed, and just memories of our basic instincts. Museum memorabilia display the negative results of caustic behavior. The ports restrictive technologies are designed to recognize corrosive, parasitic intent and shut down.

Every precaution is taken to ensure the Cosmic Port network can never be used by aggressors with harmful intentions. The first NARA ports will be sent to the most known remote locations. The expansion of the Port system is endless, nowhere is beyond the reach of this ever-escalating plan.

The arrival of the Gateway shuttle into Mockery so many years ago has become the largest social experiment since the forming of the United States back in seventeen-seventy-six. The only elements that have contributed to the magical rise and success of Queen Sparkle and the Collective Crown, is the continual challenges of both the mind and spirit. There has been one focal point or goal after another to band the populace together. Celebrating major successes as a society has brought everyone together.

The capturing of independence to make others in-dependence of the Crown has only worked because of positive common goals. At any point rebellion, or unrest could have turned into destruction, or the warring between one faction, or region, or difference to another. There are many reasons for civilization to quarrel un-necessarily; thankfully

Queen Sparkle is wise enough to not poke the bear, to not shake the jar, but gently steer the aggregate towards common denominators.

The facts are, the un-intentional social experiment in Mockery could have gone many ways, even the United States social experiment got hijacked after a period. What works best for most of the beings being governed? Any laws should apply to the governments, letting them know the limits of their power, they are the servants of the governed and not the rulers.

Creating a cryptograph of ethics defining the guidelines of contact with other species is needed to keep from causing harm. The expansion of mankind, introducing new influences is equivalent to the Ponderers entangling others without full closure of the results. Free will and self-determination are key elements in respecting others. Following Natural law and logic will serve as the template for any guide of ethics.

Being a Positive influence is the go-all, intervening when needed to save life or cure illness is a high purpose. The beings from Ricochet/ Yikes will be forever grateful for alien intervention. Beyond being a galactic fire department and rescue service, the entanglement council hopes to bring value through the interstellar Port network.

The discussions are just beginning and will remain elastic, so the Gateway shuttle was now ready to leave. The crew is much larger for the return to the Sol Earth Octa-port. With King Zero staying behind the original crew enlisted a diverse crew, Flow, Bright, Aqua, Tap, WOW, Wabble, Crys, Trio, and Quasi have volunteered to sail the cosmic network as the Gateway crew.

The Gateway shuttle is maneuvered into Port seven for the daring teleportation that will take them home. Synchronized intentions were accomplished with remote viewing and the Gateway vanishes, re-appearing in port seven of the Sol Earth Octa-port. Everyone cheered at the successful galactic jump, these teleportation's would soon become an ordinary event.

The shuttle exits the Octa-port and docks in the Starship Neuron's loading docks where it vanished from years ago. A  welcoming crowd was there to greet them, the shuttle and crew were scanned for foreign matter, after a thorough diagnosis they exit the ship to cheers and applause.

Albert, with his family and soul group hugged their old friends Seth and Shawna while anxiously awaiting meeting the new arrivals from across the galaxy. The whole world was engrossed in the story unfolding on the Starship.

Aqua was the star of the crew, although the rest of the new crew were equally amazing. Flow and Tap, the first Ponderer avatar constructs created by the Pond consciousness, Flow is the miracle mother of baby Aqua. Bright the illuminator, vibrational father, shaping reality with cosmic frequencies that are capable of reshaping realism. Crys, the crystal being, is the new science officer with the ability to assimilate data at a rate even the NARA master computer Artificial intelligence cannot match. WOW the Pople teleporter who has braved the challenges of inter planetary teleportation to help save an entire race of beings. Wabble, the Ricochet/ Yikes hero who has confronted the fears of demise to save his fellow beings and test the Octa-port safety. Finally is the paradigm breaker, Quasi, the mental stoppage clearer and his cosmic plunger Swoosh.

Everything has come full circle. The Gateway shuttle has returned at last. This may seem like the end of the story, it is just the beginning of millions of other stories, not to mention all the stories that are untold within this story. For those of you that have skipped to the last page to see how the story ends, you missed all the fun.

www.ingramcontent.com/pod-product-compliance
Lightning Source LLC
Chambersburg PA
CBHW040804120726

48005CB00012B/1297